Books by Raye Morgan

Silhouette Romance

Roses Never Fade #427
Promoted—To Wife! #1451
The Boss's Baby Mistake #1499
Working Overtime #1548
She's Having My Baby! #1571
A Little Moonlighting #1595
†*Jack and the Princess* #1655
†*Betrothed to the Prince* #1667
†*Counterfeit Princess* #1672
††*The Boss, the Baby and Me* #1751

Silhouette Books

Wanted: Mother
"The Baby Invasion"

†*Royal Nights*

Silhouette Desire

Embers of the Sun #52
Summer Wind #101
Crystal Blue Horizon #141
A Lucky Streak #393
Husband for Hire #434
Too Many Babies #543
Ladies' Man #562
In a Marrying Mood #623
Baby Aboard #673
Almost a Bride #717
The Bachelor #768
Caution: Charm at Work #807
Yesterday's Outlaw #836
The Daddy Due Date #843
Babies on the Doorstep #886
Sorry, the Bride Has Escaped #892
*Baby Dreams #997
*A Gift for Baby #1010
**Babies by the Busload* #1022
*Instant Dad #1040
Wife by Contract #1100
The Hand-Picked Bride #1119
Secret Dad #1199

†Catching the Crown
††Boardroom Brides
*The Baby Shower

RAYE MORGAN

has spent almost two decades, while writing over fifty novels, searching for the answer to that elusive question: Just what is that special magic that happens when a man and a woman fall in love? Every time she thinks she has the answer, a new wrinkle pops up, necessitating another book! Meanwhile, after living in Holland, Guam, Japan and Washington, D.C., she currently makes her home in Southern California with her husband and two of her four boys.

CHIVAREE, TEXAS

Theodore McLaughlin and Hiram Allman founded the town of Chivaree in the late nineteenth century and have been feuding ever since. It's the high-and-mighty McLaughlin ranchers pitted against the black-sheep Allman Enterprises entrepreneurs!

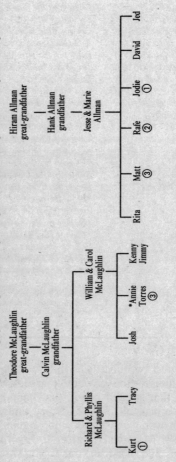

*Illegitimate
Daughter

1—*The Boss, the Baby and Me* (SR #1751, January 2005)
2—*Trading Places with the Boss* (SR#1759, March 2005)
3—*The Boss's Special Delivery* (SR#1766, May 2005)

Chapter One

The man had to go.

Jodie Allman glared at Kurt McLaughlin, head of the marketing department of Allman Industries, as he went on talking earnestly to Mabel Norton. Office hours were long over and Mabel was on her way home, her handbag slung over her shoulder. Kurt didn't glance Jodie's way as he conversed with the director of Hospitality Services, but she knew that *he* knew she was standing there across the office floor, waiting for further instructions.

"One…two…three…" she whispered to herself, tapping her foot as she counted. Counting to ten was a primitive but well-honored way of keeping control of her temper. It was probably time she moved on to more sophisticated methods—such as finding a way to get the man out of her life.

"It's such a simple thing," she told herself for the hundredth time that week, pushing her thick, blond hair back behind her ear in a gesture of impatience. "My father owns this company. Why the heck can't I get him to announce one particular layoff?"

Of course, she hadn't actually tried. Thinking about having Kurt thrown out on his ear was infinitely satisfying. But actually watching him pack up his meager belongings in a cardboard box and carry them sadly to his truck while the female support staff sobbed helplessly and shot daggers at Jodie would be another thing entirely. She wasn't nearly the tough-as-nails independent woman she would like to pretend.

The frustrating thing was, it really seemed that no one else could see through Kurt McLaughlin the way she could. Even the others in her family didn't seem to take the threat he posed seriously. And all her coworkers around here adored him. The fact that he was over six feet tall with a build right out of a woman's fantasy and a face handsome enough to turn heads in the cafeteria didn't hurt. The auburn hair that always looked a little wind-ruffled, and the green eyes that seemed to scan a woman right down to her heart and soul, were added attractions that muddied the waters for most females. They were so busy being bowled over by his admitted charms that they didn't notice what he was up to.

She'd only been back in town and working for him for

a few weeks, but she'd gotten his number right away. Once you realized what his game was, it was just so obvious.

Suddenly she noticed he was looking up at her, though he was still talking to Mabel. And to her astonishment, he was crooking his finger in her direction. Crooking his finger!

Well, that did it. There was no way she was dashing up, like a little, woolly dog, to a man who crooked his finger at her. She wasn't going to wait around any longer, either. It was way past time to go home. The three of them were probably the only people left in this ancient building, as it was. With one last baleful look in his direction, she turned on her heel and strode for the elevator, heading back up to her office to get her things.

"Hey."

It took her a moment to realize he was coming after her. Quickly, she jabbed at the Close Door button, and the doors began to move. But he was too fast for her, stepping into the elevator, and reaching across her to jab at the "stop" button. She hit the Close Door button again, just for emphasis, and he turned to grin at her as the doors opened, closed and opened again, before finally grounding together with a screeching of gears.

His grin faded fast.

"Uh-oh," he said, turning to look at the control panel.

The elevator shot up a dozen feet or so, then shuddered to a stop, complaining loudly.

"Uh-oh," Jodie echoed, agreeing with him for the first time in recent memory.

An eerie silence reigned while they both stared at the control panel, hoping for a sign of life. Then Kurt sprang forward and tried one button after another, getting absolutely no response. Alarmed, Jodie stepped forward, as well, and did the same, pushing every button twice. There was absolutely no indication that the buttons were connected to anything.

"Look what you did," Kurt muttered darkly. "We're stuck."

"What *I* did?" she responded, throwing him a smoldering glare. "You're the one who forced your way onto my elevator ride."

"I had to do that. You were trying to escape."

"Escape!" she choked, as she fought back the retort she was tempted to make. She took a deep breath.

Calm. We must remain calm. This is, after all, your current boss. Such as he may be.

"I was standing there waiting for you, trying to catch your attention for ages, but you were talking away to Mabel Norton as though it was the most important thing you'd done all day."

"It was. The most important thing in my world, at any rate." His face softened. "I was getting some advice on finding child care for Katy."

"Oh." She winced, knowing only too well how he felt about his young daughter.

"I've been having some trouble finding someone to

care for her during the day." His look sharpened. "You wouldn't happen to know anyone who might like a baby-sitting job, would you?"

She backed away, hands out. "Sorry. I don't know much about babies. Or about those who like to care for them, for that matter."

"Yes, I realized you weren't big on babies from the first," he said dryly.

That startled her a bit. She didn't know what she'd done to give him that impression, and something about the unemotional way he'd put it made her uncomfortable. But let's face it, babies made her uncomfortable.

Still, that was hardly the point. They had larger problems at the moment. Here they were, caught together in an old elevator in a building that should have been torn down years ago. But it was considered a historic landmark by the mavens of this Texas cow-country town of Chivaree. Things like this just didn't happen. Did they?

It seemed they did. But everything had been a little out of whack ever since she'd returned to her hometown after an absence of almost ten years and found a McLaughlin in a position at Allman Industries that she never would have expected a McLaughlin to have. And then she'd been told she'd be working for him. That had certainly gone against the grain.

She'd grown up thinking of all McLaughlins as the elitist enemy, the rich people up on the hill, looking down their noses at the Allmans and their ilk. Yes, "ilk" had been a word she'd heard used about her family.

She'd never been too clear on what it meant, but she did know it was a way of being condescending toward her kind. And she knew enough about some pretty unsavory incidents in the far past that had poisoned relations between the two clans—and probably always would.

Throughout her childhood, the Allmans had always been scrambling for pennies while the McLaughlins were happily buying up the entire town. There had been times when her family might even have skimmed the edges of the law just a bit here and there. But knowing that had only hardened the resentment she'd felt when others in this town whispered that the Allmans were a shiftless rabble always out for a fast buck.

And now, miraculously, the tables had turned. Her father, Jesse Allman, had somehow managed to make a go of a business, to the surprise of even his own children. In fact, his winery had grown so quickly, it was now the major employer in town. Not many people insulted him to his face these days but prejudices weren't easy to overcome. She had a good idea what the folks of Chivaree really thought about her family.

And she thought she knew what Kurt McLaughlin's true agenda was, since she'd found him happily ensconced in the management of her father's company when she had returned. Of all people—why did it have to be him? She turned back to look at the man and found him on the intercom, trying to find help.

"Hello. Hello! We're stuck in the elevator."

They both listened for a long moment, but there was

no answer. He turned and looked at her. "There's no one in the utility room," he said, frowning.

"Obviously," she agreed, trying not to think about the fact that there was probably no one at all left in the building but the two of them. Mabel Norton would have headed for the parking lot the moment Kurt dashed off toward the elevator. And everyone else had gone long ago. Their only hope was to find a way to communicate to the outside world. "Isn't there an alarm?"

"An alarm. Of course." He reached for it, pulling the lever out. Nothing happened.

"Maybe you pulled it too slowly," she said, starting to feel real apprehension seeping in. "Try it again. Give it a good jerk."

He tried again then turned to her, the lever dangling from his fingers. "Oops," he said.

She bit her lip and forced back the comment that would have been only natural at a time like this. "Well then," she said carefully, avoiding his gaze. "Since neither of us seems to have a cell phone handy, I guess we'll just have to wait."

"Wait?" He ran a hand through his thick, auburn hair, staring at her as though he thought she might really know the answer. "Wait for what?"

"For someone to realize we're missing."

He turned away impatiently, then turned back and met her dark gaze with his own brilliant one. "Everyone's gone home," he said gruffly, as though he'd just realized that fact.

She gulped. He was right. They could be here for a long time. This was not good.

"We're stuck here until someone tries to use the elevator and it doesn't arrive," he said, making the obvious deduction. "It's just you and me, kid."

In her wildest dreams, she'd never imagined a more unexpected scenario. She reached out to steady herself against the side railing. Suddenly the air seemed too thick, and his shoulders seemed too wide, looming in her way as they filled the elevator car. And in his well-tooled cowboy boots, he seemed even taller than his normally imposing height.

"This is your worst nightmare, isn't it?" He appeared to be a mind reader among his other annoying talents, though he'd said it with a hint of amusement in his voice.

"I don't know what you're talking about," she said primly, concentrating on the inspection certificate on the wall. The official-looking document claimed all was well with this horrible machine. The document was lying.

"Don't you?" He laughed softly.

She risked a look at him and immediately regretted it. "Are you trying to tell me that you enjoy being stuck in an elevator?" she demanded.

He considered her question for a moment, one eyebrow raised. "That's not as easy to answer as you might think," he told her. "Circumstances could be the deciding factor. After all, if I was stuck with Willy from the mailroom, he'd whip out a deck of cards, and we'd be playing gin so hard we would forget about the time. Or if it was Bob from Accounting, he'd be telling me fascinating stories about his time in the Special Forces during Desert Storm. And Tiana from the art department might give me a demonstration of the new belly dancing classes she's been taking."

Jodie made a sound of impatience, hoping to keep him from going on with this. "Yes, but you're not stuck with all those wonderful, interesting people. You're stuck with me."

"Yes, you." His white teeth flashed in an impudent grin, and his gaze ran up and down the length of her, making her wish she hadn't worn the snug, blue sweater and tight, denim skirt that showed off her figure with maybe just a bit too much flare. Then he challenged her teasingly. "So what are *you* good for?"

She wanted to turn and flounce off, but that was impossible under the circumstances. A flounce like that would land her smack up against the opposite wall. So she settled for trying to look bored with it all.

"Nothing, I guess," she said, letting a tiny hint of sarcasm curdle her tone.

When he leaned his long, muscular body against the wall, her gaze was magnetically drawn to the sleek slacks molded tightly across his thighs.

"Come on, Jodie," he said. "Don't sell yourself short. The way I see it, you're certainly good for a laugh."

That startled her, and she looked at him quickly, ready to resent whatever he had to say. "What are you talking about?"

He shrugged. "Your stock in trade, of course. The McLaughlin-Allman feud. You carry it around on your shoulders as though it were still 1904, and I just stole your father's favorite broodmare."

She drew herself up. Now he was really treading on her territory. "It's the *Allman-McLaughlin* feud," she said, correcting him icily. "And I have no idea why you think it's a factor in my life."

"Oh, yes, you do." His gaze hardened and he moved restlessly. "You're one of the few, you know. Most around here have given up on it."

"That's what you think." She wished she could recall the words the moment they left her lips. Because the trouble was, she was afraid what he'd said might be true. She did seem to be one of the few who remembered the feud. What had happened to it, anyway? When she'd lived here growing up, it pervaded life in this town like nothing else had.

"So that's it, isn't it?" he said. "That's what's had you treating me like someone you need to watch around the silverware. You just can't get past the whole feud."

She gave up all pretense. "Neither can any of us," she said stoutly.

"That's not true. Look at me."

She didn't want to look at him. Looking at him was likely to get her into a lot of trouble. But she did it anyway.

And for the first time, she really saw him as the others did—not as an underhanded opponent in a quarrel that had its roots in her ancestral background, but as a man who had a really engaging grin and a dynamic presence crackling with potent masculinity. And her body reacted so intensely that her heart started to race and a quiver snaked its way down her spine. When their eyes met for a beat too long, she had the unsettling feeling he really could see inside her heart and soul.

"So you think you've changed everything?" she said, hoping he didn't notice the breathlessness in her voice.

"No." He shook his head. "No, I didn't change everything. When you come right down to it, your father was the one who changed everything."

"By hiring you, you mean?"

"Sure. I guess you know they weren't exactly cheering him in the street at the time."

He said it as though he admired Jesse Allman for crossing the line. Jodie looked up at him in consternation. Did he really think her father had done that out of the goodness of his crusty ole heart? Was he really that clueless?

No, that wasn't it; he wasn't stupid. But neither was she. She'd known from the first that Kurt had an agenda of his own. Why else would he be here, working at Allman Industries, charming the heck out of everyone in sight? He could pretend all he wanted that the past was the furthest thing from his mind. She knew better. She knew McLaughlins. It had been a McLaughlin who had almost ruined her life. But that was another story.

Still, knowing what McLaughlin men were like

meant she knew she had to get away from Kurt's influence. Taking a step into the center of the elevator, she put her hands on her hips and looked around her.

"Enough of this. I think we ought to concentrate on how we're going to get the heck out of here."

He watched her lazily. "Get out of here, eh? Great idea. What exactly do you suggest?"

"Well…" She scanned the walls and the ceiling, then saw something interesting. "Look up there. Isn't that a trapdoor to the top of the elevator unit? Maybe we could open it. Shouldn't you climb up there and see?"

She looked at him expectantly. He gave her a quizzical look, still lounging against the wall, giving every indication of being perfectly content to stay right where he was. "Me?"

"Why not *you?*" she asked a bit impatiently. "Don't men always do that in movies?"

He looked up at the supposed opening, which was more than two feet over his head, and nodded. "Sure. In movies." Looking back down, he favored her with a caustic look. "Just exactly how do you picture me getting up there? Am I supposed to sprout wings, or pull out my suction shoes for wall-walking?" He cocked an eyebrow when she didn't answer. "Pole-vault, maybe?"

She licked her lips and frowned. "I don't know. How do those men in the movies usually do it?"

He shrugged. "I could try climbing on your shoulders," he suggested mildly. "Other than that, I don't see a way up."

She didn't bother to roll her eyes, though she certainly felt like doing so. "There must be some way," she muttered, frowning as she gazed about for inspiration.

He went back to looking at the small trapdoor. "And once I got up there," he mused, "who knows what sort of electrical wiring is lurking on the other side of the door, just waiting to fry the unsuspecting adventurer." He turned to look at her with amusement. "Tell you what. I could probably lift *you* up to the opening. How about you climbing up there and seeing what can be done?"

"Are you crazy?"

He shrugged as though he were disappointed in her response. "Give the woman a chance to be a hero, and what does she do?" he murmured.

"We don't need a hero," she retorted. "What we need is some competence."

"Ouch. I suppose you consider that a direct hit."

"No. A glancing blow, maybe." She sighed, shoulders sagging. Verbal jousting with the man was all very well, but it wasn't going to get her out of the situation. "Look, I know climbing up out of this thing is probably not doable. But it's just so frustrating being stuck here. Can't you think of anything?"

His green eyes flickered with something she couldn't quite identify, but he spoke calmly. "I believe in trying to make the best of any given predicament," he said. "So I look at this as worthwhile. It's a good opportunity for us to get better acquainted."

"Better acquainted!" She gaped at him. "I don't

need to be better acquainted with you. I've known you all my life."

He shook his head. "Not true."

She threw out her hands, palms up. "What do you call knowing you from birth?"

"You've known *of* me. You haven't really known me. And I haven't known you." He gave her a slow smile. "We've been like ships passing in the night, existing side by side, but hardly paying any attention to one another. We need to get to know each other a little more intimately."

There was something in the way he said that which caused her to take a quick step backward. From her new position of security in the corner of the elevator car, she gazed at him levelly. Was this all part of his plan? Was he trying to subvert her the way he'd done with the rest of the people around here?

"I don't think we need to know each other better at all. We've got a nice, cool working relationship. Professional and businesslike. Let's leave it at that."

"Is that really what you think we have?" he asked innocently. "I thought we had a thing going where I was the boss and you were the recalcitrant, embittered employee who was always second-guessing her management."

That about nailed it, she had to admit. She lifted her chin defiantly. "Is that a problem for you?"

He laughed. "No, it's not a problem. A diversion, perhaps, but not a problem." His expression changed. "And I guess it gives you the illusion of keeping the flame going on our families' blasted feud, doesn't it?"

She wasn't going to answer that, and he knew it. Instead of prodding her, he opened a new topic.

"So tell me, Jodie. Why did you come back?"

She knew what he was asking. It was a question everyone who moved back to Chivaree got at one time or another. Most people were astonished that someone would come back to this dusty town after having made good their getaway. She decided to be frank about it.

"I came back because Matt showed up on my doorstep one day and told me that I had to."

Matt was her brother, the oldest in her family. He was even a few years older than Kurt.

"Had to?" he echoed back to her in disbelief. "And you did what someone else told you to do without a qualm?" He shook his head in wonder. "I'll have to ask him what his secret is."

She lifted her chin. "He made a compelling case."

He nodded slowly. "I see. And then you showed up in Chivaree, arrived at the office to go to work and found out you were going to have to work for me, at least for the short run."

"Yes."

"That must have been one of your darker days."

She turned and glared at him, stung by the way he was continually making fun of her. "Will you stop? It's not permanent. I'll be moving on to some other department in a month or so." It was her father's brilliant plan that she should sample each area of the business to get a solid foundation in the company. "In the meantime, I can handle it."

"Can you?" An expression of wary skepticism crossed his handsome face. "You give every indication of hating every minute of our precious time together."

"I do not." She bit her tongue. If she wasn't careful, this could turn into a silly shouting match. A new tack was called for. She took a deep breath and started on one. "But you left town before I did. Why did *you* come back?"

She'd heard the cover story, that his wife had died and left him with their baby, so he'd returned to where his extended family could help him take care of the child. But she had her doubts. And wasn't he hunting around for someone to baby-sit his daughter? That pretty much gave the lie to that excuse.

No, Kurt McLaughlin had an agenda. She was pretty sure she had a clue what it might be, too. And she could bet it had something to do with ruining things for the Allmans. After all, that was the pattern set over a hundred years ago by their great-grandfathers. The McLaughlins were always supposed to win, and the Allmans were always supposed to end up with their faces in the dirt.

"Okay, I'll tell you why I came back," he said slowly, turning his face and staring at the wall. "Believe it or not, I came back because I love this old town."

"What?" She gaped at him.

Chivaree was not one of those adorable little towns people wrote songs about. Things had improved lately, but it was still a windswept, dusty place that the inter-state bypassed years ago. People didn't flock to Chiva-ree. People cashed in their chips and headed out for brighter lights as soon as they could scrape together the carfare.

From what she'd heard, he'd spent a good number of years in New York City. She'd noticed that his voice still had a nice Texas drawl, but it was subtle. So he hadn't gone completely citified.

"It's true," he went on, his voice low and gravelly. "And when things seemed to fall apart for me out there in the big world, the only thing I could think of was coming back to Chivaree. Coming home."

Coming home to heal was the feeling implicit in his voice.

For just a moment, she believed him. He sounded so sincere, and there was some sort of emotion in his face, a hint of pain, deep down. For just a flash, she bought it.

But she stopped herself quickly. He was smart, all right. He was giving her exactly the story that was most likely to touch her heart and make her believe. He was playing with her heartstrings in a very disturbing way. She had to get out of here before she fell for this stuff.

He'd turned back, and was pulling off his tie and loosening the neck of his shirt, pulling open buttons as though they were snaps. Darkly tanned skin with just a hint of chest hair appeared before her horrified gaze.

"Is it just me," he said huskily, his eyelids drooping, "or is it getting hot in here?"

Her pulse was racing. One moment, he set out the emotional trap. Now, the physical one was laid out in front of her, just waiting for her to step into it. And darn it all if her own traitorous body wasn't swooning like a lovesick puppy, even as she disdained the obvious way he was approaching her.

Turning away abruptly, she quickly changed the subject. "I'm not hot at all," she said with an emphasis he surely couldn't miss. "But I am hungry. For food," she added quickly. Glancing back, she was chagrined to see that his eyes were gleaming wickedly.

"Are you?" he responded.

She turned back to face him, chin-high. "Desperately. I skipped lunch to get those preliminary sketches out to the art department." She grimaced. "I wish I had my purse."

"Why?" He pretended to look about the car. "Is there a food machine here I missed?"

"No, I've got a candy bar in it."

"Hmm." He plunged a hand down into the pocket of his crisply tailored slacks. "Look what I found. A roll of peppermints."

"Oh." She looked at them longingly. She really was hungry, and her mouth was so dry.

"Here." He offered the roll to her after he'd popped one into his own mouth. She hesitated, but hunger overcame her inhibitions.

"Thanks," she said shortly, taking a mint and sighing as the sparkling sugar did its work.

"You see?" he said softly, as he watched her. "I'm even willing to share my last meal with you."

She started to say something. It was surely going to be a scathing retort, something that would knock him back on his heels for good. Unfortunately, the words themselves were lost to history, because the breath she took in to help facilitate her clever words shot what was left of the peppermint right down her throat. Now, instead of putting him in his place, she was choking.

"Here." A man of action, he took matters in hand immediately, giving her a couple of sharp thumps on the back. When that didn't seem to dislodge the little intruder, he turned her quickly and wrapped his arms around her from behind for the Heimlich maneuver.

"Hey," she protested with a cough, before he got in a good thrust. "Stop! I'm okay."

He relaxed, but for some reason his arms didn't remove themselves from around her waist. "Are you sure?" he said, his voice just a bit husky, and his face so close to hers, she could feel his warm breath on her neck.

"Yes, I'm sure." She pushed against him, but he didn't release her. "Kurt, let go!"

Turning her head, she met his gaze. And then something magical happened. It wasn't just that she suddenly noticed the golden flecks in his green eyes. It wasn't even the electric sizzle that began to spread everywhere his body was touching hers. But suddenly she was filled with a longing so deep, so overwhelming, it took her breath away. She wanted to be kissed. She wanted to be kissed by Kurt McLaughlin.

"Oh," she said softly, like a woman in a trance, her gaze fixed on his generous mouth. She tilted her head, her own lips parted, a yearning coursing through her. And for just a moment, she was sure it was going to happen.

And then he was pulling away, leaving her tottering off balance and feeling as though he'd thrown cold water on her. Feeling like a fool.

At least he didn't laugh at her. Shooting back his cuff, he looked at his wristwatch, suddenly all business.

"Oh, dammit, it is getting late. I'm way overdue for picking Katy up. We'd better get some help so we can get out of here."

Reaching behind her, she steadied herself with a hand on the railing. What was he saying? "Get some help?" she asked him, still breathless and embarrassed. "What are you talking about?"

Flipping back the tail of his suit coat, he pulled out something that had been attached to his belt. Staring openmouthed, Jodie saw a cell phone in his hand.

"I'll just make a call," he said innocently. "Hope the battery is still good. If so, we'll get out of here in no time."

She shook her head and blinked to clear her mind, then gave a sound of outrage. "You mean you've had that with you *this whole time?*" she cried. "Why didn't you say so when I asked?"

"You never actually *asked* if I had one—you just assumed I didn't," he murmured. He opened the phone and began punching in a number. "Hi, Jasper? Sorry to bother you, but we've got a problem here at the office. I'm going to have to ask you to come back in and help me get out of the elevator."

Murder. That was what was called for here. Something quick and painless, when he wasn't looking. No jury in the world would convict her. Groaning, she closed her eyes and clenched her fists at her side. If she hadn't despised him before, she now had plenty of reason to start.

But that was his plan, wasn't it? Abruptly, she opened her eyes again and glared at his pleased smile. Something had to be done about this man!

Chapter Two

Jodie sat back and looked at her family, gathered around the big, antique kitchen table where they had come together for generations. Funny how it felt so familiar and yet so strange. The main thing missing was her mother, who had died of cancer when Jodie was sixteen. Her little brother Jed was also absent, the only family member Matt and Rita hadn't managed to find and hog-tie to bring back home.

Rita had cooked an excellent meal—as she always did—of chicken and dumplings in the old style. Jodie glanced down the table at where her sister sat. She watched affectionately as the older woman blew a strand of hair back out of her eyes and looked expectantly from one person to another at the table, obviously trying to gauge how they liked what they were eating. When her gaze met her sister's, she favored her with a warm smile. At least one good thing had come out of all this. Rita was happy to have most of the family together again.

Rita took care of the house and the family the way their mother would have if she hadn't died twelve years before. She was a wonderful homemaker, and she deserved to have a loving man in her life and a family of her own. Unfortunately, you didn't meet many great, unattached men at the meat counter at the Chivaree supermarket these days. And Rita didn't often veer much farther from home than that.

Matt had been her partner in reuniting the family. But Matt didn't look happy, the way Rita did. Matt was the oldest male child in the family. He was the one who had shown up on Jodie's doorstep, in Dallas, a month before and talked her into coming back home, giving her a long spiel about how they all needed to pull together now that their father was ill. These days, he seemed to care about that almost as much as Rita did.

In many ways, Matt had been Jodie's original role model. After all, he'd been the first to defy their father and leave town, heading for medical school in Atlanta. He'd worked for years in a large urban hospital, and now he was back in his dumpy little hometown. She noted the brooding look on his handsome face and wondered what had put it there. Something was bothering him. She had no idea what it was.

But she didn't have to worry about things like that with her sunny brother David, the one she looked the most like. They both had blond hair and brown eyes and a sprinkling of freckles over short noses.

Sitting next to Matt and eating everything he could get on his plate with youthful enthusiasm, David was the one who had never really left. Someone had asked her just the other day why such a handsome, happy-go-lucky young man who looked like he should be on a surfboard in Malibu would stay in Chivaree when there was a whole world out there for him. She'd laughed and said he was too lazy to leave. But that wasn't true. She supposed she might be the only one who knew the real reason why he stayed. Love made people do strange things sometimes.

And then there was dark-eyed Rafe, the brother who was the same age as Kurt McLaughlin, the one now looking at her with a penetrating gaze that said, *Hey, Jodie, don't try to con me. I can see right through this polite little act you're putting on. I can read your mind.*

She stared right back at him with a half smile, hoping he got the message. *Mind your own business!*

"Hey, Pop," David said, greeting their father as he entered the room. "You going to try to eat something?"

Leaning on his cane, the gray-haired man shook his head as Rita jumped up to pull out a chair for him. "No. I can't eat anything. I just wanted to come out and sit with you all and look at your faces." He sat down heavily, then made a scan of the table. "My pride and joy," he muttered in a tone that could have been loving, but sounded a little sarcastic.

Glancing at him and then away, Jodie felt a stew of conflicting emotion—love, resentment, anger, pity. What could you do when you disliked your own parent almost as much as you loved him?

"So you all came back to save the farm for the old man, eh?" He laughed softly. "I guess I raised myself a bunch of good ones after all."

"Hey, Pop," Rafe said, leaning forward. "I was talking to our Dallas distributor today. Looks like we might have a shot at getting a contract with the whole Wintergreen Store chain. That could be huge for us."

Jesse Allman nodded, but he wasn't looking at Rafe. His gaze was trained on his oldest son. He'd been trying to get Matt to fulfill the role of heir apparent in the business for years, without a lot of success. Though Matt had often helped out in the old days when all they had was the tiny, struggling Allman Winery, he'd been away at college when Jesse had developed the plan to become the distributor for all the little wineries of this part of Texas hill country. That had launched all the success, and it was no secret Jesse thought Matt ought to be involved. "You got a dog in this fight, Matt?" he asked.

Matt looked surprised. "What about?"

"This Wintergreen thing."

Matt shrugged. "It's up to you, Pop. You know I'm not into the business side of things."

Jesse's eyes narrowed. "You oughta be," he said shortly.

Matt and Rafe exchanged glances. "Talk to Rafe," Matt said calmly. "He's the one who knows what's going on."

Jodie sighed. It was the same old story. Did nothing ever change? The Allman family business had grown larger, morphing into Allman Industries, and the Allman family had gotten richer, changing from the old scruffy bunch who seemed to skim along just this side of law-breaking into this vaguely respectable family that provided a good chunk of the local jobs. But the old emotions still simmered just below the surface. She was beginning to wonder if it hadn't been a big mistake for her to come back.

"What's eatin' you, missy?" her father said, looking at her accusingly. "You still trying to get me to get rid of that McLaughlin boy?"

Jodie winced and put a napkin to her lips. "I never said I wanted you to get rid of him," she protested. "I just want you to be aware of the danger he poses."

"Danger?"' David looked up with a grin. "Ole Kurt McLaughlin? He's a pussycat."

"I don't trust the McLaughlins any more than you do," Matt chimed in. "But I've got to admit, Kurt is doing a fine job with marketing. We're lucky to have him."

She glanced quickly around the table, realizing with a sense of astonishment that she didn't have anyone on her side at all. Not one of them understood how danger-ous it was to let a man like Kurt into the power struc-ture of their family business.

"I know your game, missy." Jesse grinned at his daughter. "You're like me. You can't forget or forgive." He slapped the flat of his hand down on the table. "But I'm not getting rid of him. Hell, no. He's good at what he does. I don't care if he is a McLaughlin. In fact, I love that he's a McLaughlin. I love the looks on their pompous faces when I'm in town, or at the chamber of commerce meetings. I can smile at them and say, 'Your fair-haired boy is workin' for me now. Because I'm the one who's making it in this town. You McLaughlins are done for.'"

She was reminded of all the reasons why she'd run away from this man in the first place, when she was a rebellious eighteen-year-old. She'd planned never to come back. And she might have stuck to that plan if Matt hadn't found her and talked her into coming home again.

"He's old, Jodie," Matt had told her earnestly. "Old and sick. He needs us. All of us."

She noticed with a start that her father's hands were shaking, and her gaze flew to his face, searching for evidence. To her surprise, her heart began to race with something close to fear. Matt was right. He *was* old and sick. She might still be angry with him for things he'd done in the past, but he was still her father and, deep down, she cared for him. Okay, it was good that she'd come home. And despite everything, she had to stay, at least for a while.

And that meant she had to deal with Kurt McLaughlin. A memory sailed into her head of how it had felt with his arms around her in the elevator car, and she almost gasped aloud. She definitely had to harden herself to his lethal charm. She was stuck working for him, and maybe that was for the best. After all, somebody had to look out for the good of the family.

An hour later, she escaped from the tensions in the house and took a brisk walk toward the newly renovated downtown. The sky was velvet-blue, with a full moon rising. The air was warm and dry. She could smell newly cut hay somewhere nearby.

She'd paced these same streets when she was eighteen and trying to figure out what she was going to do. And just around the corner was the little park where she and Jeremy used to meet secretly to plot how they were going to escape from Chivaree together. That seemed so long ago.

Jeremy. Had she ever really loved him? When she looked back now, she saw more excitement than love. They had needed each other for support at the time. But that wasn't really true. She'd needed him. It turned out he hadn't needed her at all. But that was always the way with the McLaughlins, wasn't it?

Her steps slowed as she reached Cabrillo, the main street. The area was less familiar now, with new storefronts on some of the buildings, and a few new structures housing a boutique and a crafts store. It was good to see the town looking prosperous, she supposed, though it did give her a twinge to see how things had changed.

Millie's Café was just ahead, and that looked exactly the same. Maybe she would go in and have a cup of coffee and say hello to Millie, the mother of Shelley, her best friend in high school. Lights from the café spilled out onto the sidewalk, and Jodie began to anticipate how warm it was going to be once she'd gone in and snuggled into her old favorite booth.

But as she neared the corner, she got a glimpse of the people inside. It startled her to discover the place was packed. There were people crowding the entryway, waiting for seats, while others filled the booths, and still more sat at the counter. For a fraction of a moment, she got a flashing glimpse of a man who looked enough like Kurt to make her heart jump in dismay. Not wanting another possible run-in with that infuriating man, she just kept walking.

Darn! Was she really going to spend all her time reacting to Kurt? She couldn't live this way. Looking back over her shoulder, trying to see if that really was him inside the café, she stepped off the curb and started across the street.

The thing was, there had never been a stoplight on that corner when she'd lived in Chivaree before. There had never been enough traffic to warrant one. Somehow, it hadn't registered with her that there was one there now.

Brakes screeched. Fear flashed through her and she looked up, frozen for a few seconds. Then, she jumped, her whole body moving in a twitch reflex that somehow got her out of the way. But at the same time, her mind processed the fact that Kurt couldn't be in Millie's Café because that was Kurt's face behind the wheel.

Kurt! After veering to miss her, he tried to regain control of his vehicle. And she watched in horror as his truck swerved just enough to get caught by a car coming in the other direction. There was a smash, a crunch, the horrifying shriek of metal in distress.

It wasn't much more than a fender bender, but Jodie ran forward, apprehension flashing through her system, her heart in her throat. The driver of the car jumped out, swearing. But Kurt didn't move. Dread building, Jodie yanked at the handle on the truck door. It came open, and she stared at the contorted way Kurt's body lay in the cab. She gasped, and his green eyes opened.

"Hi," he said, his wide mouth twisted, obviously in pain. "Uh, Jodie? Think you could call the paramedics? Something's wrong with my leg."

She was doomed, that was all there was to it. Every time she turned around, there was Kurt McLaughlin, interfering with her peace of mind. It was enough to make her want to scream.

Or at least complain a bit. But how could you complain about a man when you'd just crippled him?

Looking at him lying in his bed in the cozy house he shared with his baby daughter, Katy, she swallowed hard and wished she were anywhere else. Her brother Matt was using an automatic sander gizmo to smooth out a rough spot in the fiberglass cast he'd applied at the

town clinic an hour or so before. Her brother David, who
had helped get Kurt home, was standing around with his
hands shoved down in the pockets of his jeans, looking
very amused with it all. And she was standing in the
shadows, between the bookcase and the closet, wishing
the earth would open and swallow her whole.

"I knew Jodie had it in for me," Kurt drawled, his
voice half teasing, but with just enough of an edge to
set her nerves twitching. "I just didn't realize how far
she was prepared to go."

She moaned softly, but David couldn't resist expand-
ing on the joke.

"You know, sis, if you really want to take a guy out,
you're supposed to be the one in the car. He should be
the one in the street, running for his life."

She ignored him. She'd spent too many years fend-
ing off the pestering of big brothers—she knew better
than to rise to the bait. Besides, she did feel terrible for
what had happened, and she wanted to make sure Kurt
knew it.

"I just don't know how I could have been so stupid,"
she began, and not for the first time.

Kurt looked up at her and groaned. "Jodie, if you try
to tell me how sorry you are one more time, I'm going
to have your brother use that surgical tape on your
mouth."

"We'd have to tape up her hands, too, or she'd be
using them to give you apologies in sign language,"
Matt said with a smirk.

"Do that, and she'll have to resort to tapping out her pleas for forgiveness in Morse code with the toes of her shoes," David threw in teasingly. "Let me tell you something. This sister of ours doesn't give up easily."

Jodie flushed as they all laughed. It was obvious her brothers both liked Kurt. She didn't know how they could be so blind.

But another thing that stumped her was how well Kurt had taken the whole thing. She would have expected a little snarling, a few insults about watching where she was going, and a whole lot of swearing. But there had been very little of that. Maybe if he'd been grouchier about it all, she would feel better. At least then she could get mad instead of feeling so wretched.

Kurt had wanted paramedics. She only wished she could have obliged. But there were no paramedics in Chivaree. There was Old Man Cooper, who answered the phone at the fire department and then called around to the volunteers if there was a fire. He supposedly had a little first-aid training. But he certainly wasn't competent to deal with a broken leg. So she'd called Matt. After all, he was the best physician in town as far as she was concerned. He'd come right away, bringing David with him, and between them they had carried Kurt to the clinic so that Matt could X-ray the leg.

No major bone was broken, but the patella was cracked, a situation that could be very painful and required a cast that held the knee immobile.

"We'll have to keep you in the cast for a couple of

weeks," Matt had told him. "Then we'll take it off and do some X-rays to see if you can transfer to a knee brace. That will give you a lot more freedom of movement."

It had all gone pretty smoothly. They'd brought Kurt back to his house and installed him in his bedroom, where he was right now. Matt had given Kurt some sort of painkiller when he'd worked on him. Maybe that was why Kurt seemed to be taking it so calmly. Maybe he was just groggy from the medicine.

She wanted to go home. She ached to leave this behind. But she couldn't really leave. After all, the accident had been her fault.

"Jodie is a licensed physical therapist," Matt was saying. "That will be handy. She can help in your rehabilitation."

"I'd forgotten that," Kurt said. He grinned at her, knowing it would bug her. "That will be useful."

Jodie felt numb. Everything that happened seemed to tie her more firmly to this man in one way or another. As she'd said before, she was doomed.

Matt rose to get something from his bag and, to Jodie's surprise, he stopped in front of a framed picture of a cute baby girl, that was set on the top of an antique dresser.

"This your daughter?" he asked gruffly.

Kurt looked up and nodded proudly. "Yes, that's Katy. She's at my mother's for the night."

Matt was still staring at the picture in a way Jodie found a little odd. She couldn't imagine when her big brother had become a child person. Considering that none of the six siblings in her family, including herself, were married or had children, she'd assumed they all felt pretty much the way she did. She didn't dislike children, but she felt a lot more comfortable keeping them at a distance, avoiding too much up-close-and-personal interaction. Maybe she'd been wrong about Matt.

"It's a good thing the baby wasn't with you when you had the accident," Matt said with feeling.

"Yes," Kurt agreed. "That's one blessing, at least."

Jodie agreed, though she didn't say it aloud. Just imagine if she'd been responsible for hurting Kurt's baby. She shuddered, not wanting to think about it.

Still, Matt lingered, staring at the portrait. "She's a beautiful baby," he said. "About how old?"

"Sixteen months."

"A little over one year."

"Yes."

Jodie frowned, wondering what was eating her brother. This just didn't fit with the image she had of him. Then she turned to look at Kurt lying back against the pillows, and immediately wished she hadn't. All thoughts of Matt flew out the window, and unwelcome reactions to Kurt took their place.

Since he'd put on cutoff jeans, to leave his damaged leg bare for the cast, she'd wisely been avoiding looking at his beautifully sculpted good leg, which was covered with a sleek pelt of reddish-brown hair. But while she wasn't paying attention, somehow his shirt had been removed, as well, and now he was displaying a set of sexy muscles and a washboard stomach, all wrapped up in the most deliciously smooth and bronzed skin she'd ever seen.

The man was a damn Greek god! Gazing at him made her feel dangerously warm and fuzzy inside.

Realizing with a start that she'd been staring at his powerfully built chest too long, she glanced up into his bright green eyes and saw that he'd been watching her all along. Turning ten shades of red, she spun on her heel and pretended a sudden fascination with the collection of old first editions in his bookcase.

Matt and Kurt went on talking, but she didn't hear a word they were saying. Her head was buzzing with a strange vibration, and all she could think of was that his gaze had been so full of awareness of her, it was downright scary. Awareness not only of what she was feeling, but of just what she might be thinking, as well.

Had he understood just how drawn to him she was physically? Had he known she'd ached for him to kiss her in the elevator? It was all so humiliating!

She tried some even breathing, determined to get this silly blushing under control, and to avoid meeting Kurt's eyes again. And then she took a chance and escaped into the rest of the house, taking a deep breath as she did so. The cool air in the living room was a welcome relief.

She looked around the room. It was nicely furnished in a simple style, but there were toys everywhere. She winced, looking away. Funny. It had been almost ten years, but looking at baby things still brought on a wave of nausea every time. She knew it was silly and self-destructive to let that reaction rule her life, but she hadn't found a way to fight it yet. Losing a baby was hard, even if that baby hadn't been born yet at the time.

She turned toward the bookcase, refocusing her attention with a soft sigh. She couldn't help but wonder why Kurt didn't live in the old Victorian mansion up on the hill, where the other McLaughlins congregated. If he'd really come back to get help with his daughter, you would think he would have stayed there. It was supposed to be a wonderful house.

She'd never been inside the place herself, never been invited to the parties the other girls in town had attended on Sunday afternoons. In those days, Allmans weren't welcome at anything put on by a McLaughlin.

"Hey, Jodie." David came around the corner.

She jumped, startled out of her reverie. "What is it?"

"Matt's finished."

"Oh. Good."

"But Kurt wants to talk to you alone for a few minutes before we go."

"Alone?" Her hand went instinctively to her throat. "Why? What does he want to talk to me about?"

David gave her a quizzical look. "I don't know. Work, I guess." He shrugged and turned back toward the door. "Anyway, we'll be waiting in the car."

She swallowed hard. "Okay."

She made her way back into the bedroom, cringing when she saw Kurt again, looking so helpless on the bed. "Oh, gosh, I'm really…"

"Don't say it," he ordered shortly. "I know you wish it hadn't happened. So do I. But it's done now. So forget about it."

Her eyebrows rose as she noted a change in his tone. He'd put on more clothes and abandoned the easygoing attitude. What had happened to the friendly guy who'd traded jokes with her brothers just a few moments before? But the man had just broken his patella. He had to be tired, and probably the pain was coming back. She really ought to cut him a little slack.

"What we have to do now is figure out how to deal with the aftermath," he was saying.

"The aftermath?" What was there to figure out? He had an injury. Obviously, that was going to put him at a disadvantage for awhile. It might put a crimp in his plans, but it also meant she would be able to keep tabs on him more easily, when you came right down to it.

He was nodding. "Matt says I can't go back in to work for at least two weeks."

"Oh. That's too bad." She had visions of working without him around to distract her. Her spirits brightened. Maybe things were looking up after all.

"But I'm in the middle of a couple of projects that can't wait. So I'm going to have to work at home."

"At home?" she echoed, emotions switching as she

began to get a very bad feeling about what was coming next.

"Yes. I've got a computer and a fax machine right here. I won't be able to move around a lot, though. And that's where you will come in."

"I will?"

"Sure. You can come work with me here. I'll probably get twice as much done that way. It will all be for the best."

"Oh, but…"

"I've been thinking it over. You can go in to work at your regular time, clear up anything you have to do there, then bring me anything I need to deal with and work here until lunchtime. You won't have any problem with that, will you?"

What could she say? This was her fault and she had to help him any way she could. Jodie felt her head begin to ache and she bit her lip. She foresaw long mornings working with Kurt, the two of them alone, their heads together over some sticky problem, intimacy growing…. *No! Impossible!*

"You know," she said quickly, "I think it would be better if I got Paula to come over here instead." Oh, good thinking. Paula was the typist/file clerk they used. "I'm in the middle of a few things, too, you know. I'll just stay at the office to make sure everything is covered, and Paula can run back and forth, kind of a liaison between us and…"

"That won't work."

She blinked. "Why not?"

"Because I want you here."

Exactly what she was afraid of.

His gaze was dark and fathomless, and his jaw was set. He was all boss right now. He was giving orders. The problem was, she wasn't all that good at taking orders.

She stared right back at him. "Why me?" she asked.

He frowned. "Are you, or are you not, my assistant?"

"That's temporary."

"As far as work goes, let's live in the moment. Answer the question."

She wanted to say something sassy and insubordinate but she realized it was going to seem very childish if she did that. But she was having a very hard time bending to his will too easily.

Their gazes locked and held. Jodie felt a surge of anger, but she managed to keep it reined in for the moment. Still, he could tell she was unhappy. To her surprise, that brought the amusement back into his expression.

"Do all your apologies mean nothing?" he asked her softly.

The nerve!

"And I guess you casting aside all my apologies means even less?"

He laughed softly. "Jodie, calm down. This is the way I want it. You're going to have to comply."

"Or what? You'll fire me?"

"Fire you from your father's company? Never." His

grin was lopsided in a particularly infuriating way. "I could, however, begin giving the better assignments to Paula in order to leave you time for document-copying and coffee-brewing duties."

She turned away from him, furious, and tempted to head for the door. His tone said it all. *Look at this, Jodie. You laid me low, but I'm still in control.* She didn't want to give him the satisfaction of saying she would do as he wished, though she knew she was probably going to have to. But at the same time, a small part of her glowed with satisfaction. She only wished her brothers had been there to see Kurt get autocratic with her.

You see? He is underhanded. He is out to sabotage us in some way. You just wait! I'm not wrong about that.

Come to think of it, maybe it was just as well that she would be hanging around wherever Kurt was working. After all, she was the only one who was clued in to what he was up to. Someone had to keep an eye on him.

She turned back and looked at him. "All right," she said grudgingly. "I'll be here."

To her surprise, he looked relieved rather than triumphant. But before he had a chance to say anything, she added a warning.

"Kurt, just so that we understand each other. I'll come to your house. I'll do a good job for you. I'll work with you just fine, as long…as long as you don't do anything to hurt my family."

"Hurt your family?" He was going back into his innocent act. "Why would I hurt your family?"

She threw up her hands. "Oh, I don't know. Why is there air?"

"That same old, ancient feud. Is that it?"

"Bingo. Give the man the grand prize."

"I don't want any grand prize, Jodie. All I want is you…here."

Her mouth had gone dry. What was he saying? She didn't really want to find out.

"Well, you've got it," she said flippantly, turning to go. She stopped at the door and looked back. "Remember, be careful what you ask for," she reminded him. "Things have a way of turning out differently from what you expect."

"We can always hope so," he murmured.

She hesitated, wishing she had a better grip on his meaning. He was saying things that sounded strangely suggestive, and yet she had the feeling he didn't really mean them the way she was hearing them. Could it be that he was just trying to throw her off balance?

Oh, good guess, Jodie!

Still, it wouldn't hurt to make sure.

"And there will be no…romantic relationship," she said firmly.

He stared at her for a moment, then laughed.

"Ha. Listen, Jodie. Any romancing I do from now on will be strictly recreational. My 'relationship' days are only evident in my life's rearview mirror."

The bitterness in his tone startled her, but she wasn't about to let him see that. He had issues. Why not?

Everyone had issues. At least he'd had a happy marriage at one point. Some people didn't even get that much.

"That's exactly what I'm saying. I don't do recreational."

"Then we understand each other perfectly."

If only she believed that. With one last lingering glance at the man, she made her way out the door and headed for the front of the house, feeling as though she'd just avoided a dangerous trap.

But what traps would he try to spring on her tomorrow?

Chapter Three

Jodie had it all planned out by the time she pulled up in front of Kurt's house the next morning. Cool, calm and professional. That was the way she was going to play this. Dripping with efficiency and competence, but detached. Aloof.

Almost robotlike, she promised herself as she made her way up the winding walk to the front steps. *No emotions.*

She'd arranged communications with Shelley, her best friend from childhood who also worked at Allman Industries, to keep her posted on things at the office. Then she'd slicked her thick, blond hair back in a bun, and put on slacks and a tailored cotton shirt. Her dark eyes were shaded by huge sunglasses. Impersonal. Businesslike.

The shiny green door opened before she had a chance

to knock on it. Kurt stood before her wearing the suggestion of a faintly mocking grin and not much else. He was bare-chested and his biceps were swollen with the effort of using the crutches. Baggy, cotton cutoff pajama bottoms rode low on his perfectly sculpted hips. She took the sight in and blinked in surprise, taking a half step backward.

Too much male flesh, too close and too early in the morning. The shock stopped her breath in her throat, and she choked.

"You okay?" he asked, his green eyes sparkling with shafts of light from the early morning sun.

"Oh, certainly," she replied, regaining her emotional balance quickly. "I'm just worried about you. Don't you think you might catch a cold with all that bare skin hanging out?"

"'Hanging out'?" He looked down as though alarmed. "Where? I thought I was in pretty good shape."

The evidence was irrefutable, but she pretended to consider that skeptically.

"Well, 'good' is a judgment, isn't it? I suppose you could say it was in the eye of the beholder." She glanced past him into the house. "Lose your robe somewhere?"

"Robes just get in the way. It's too much trouble trying to wear clothes and use these crutches, too." He cocked an eyebrow as though a sudden thought had crossed his mind. "Are you implying that my state of undress disturbs you?"

Her eyes narrowed. "I've worked as a physical therapist for the last five years. The human body doesn't disturb me."

That blatant lie almost brought on a flush, but she managed to hold it back. The average body might not cause a blip on her radar screen, but this particular body had her equipment going haywire. She only hoped he didn't notice. In fact, the better part of valor might be in beating a hasty retreat.

"But since you don't seem to be ready to do any work, I think I'll just run over to the office and come back later." She turned, ready to make good on her threat, but he stopped her with a soft oath.

"Cut the dramatics, Jodie," he said impatiently. "I've got plenty of things waiting for your expert attention. We don't have a lot of time to waste."

She looked back, unable to ignore the way the morning light added a wonderful patina to his bronzed skin. "We don't?"

"No. Come on in. We need to get moving here."

She frowned, suspicious, but turned back in his direction. "What exactly do you have in mind?" she asked.

His bright gaze met hers, and he smiled. Her knees almost buckled. The man's smile could melt the polar ice cap. Global warming had nothing on this guy.

"Jodie, Jodie," he was saying. "You're going to have to learn to trust me."

"Trust is something you earn," she reminded him. "Right now I would rather have the facts."

"Okay Miss Sunshine. Here are the facts, and nothing but the facts. I want to go out to the vineyards today, and since I can't really drive myself, I'm going to have to count on you to do that for me."

"The vineyards?" She looked at him in surprise. "What for?"

"I'm working up concepts for a new ad campaign, and I want to go out and get some sense of what is possible. Take some pictures. Get some ideas."

Pulling off her sunglasses, she glanced at him, then looked back more intently. His expression wasn't giving anything away, but she wondered what he was up to. "Does my father know you're going out there?" she asked.

A strange look passed over his face, then disappeared as mysteriously as it had come. "Why? Do you think I need his permission?"

She hesitated, thinking exactly that, but knowing from his tone that he wouldn't like her answer. Driving all the way out to the vineyards would take up most of the day. She thought quickly, going over things that needed her attention back at the office. There really wasn't anything that couldn't wait a day. And if he was going out there, she really ought to go along, just to keep an eye on him.

"Okay, I'll drive," she said quickly. "But…" She glanced at the toys littering the carpet. "What about your baby?"

"My mother's still got her. She already brought Katy by to say hello. I can't go a morning without a couple of baby kisses, you know." He grinned, remembering, and managed to look almost endearing. "And of course, my mother needed time to give me her daily lecture," he added mostly to himself, his smile fading.

"Lecture?" Suddenly the truth dawned on her. Why hadn't she thought of this before? "Your family doesn't like you working for Allman Industries anymore than I do, do they?"

His green eyes had a way of going opaque just when she most wanted to get a glimpse of some reaction from him. But she didn't really need to see confirmation. The McLaughlins still despised the Allmans. That was all she really needed to know.

She looked at him, with his flimsy pajama bottoms and the day's worth of beard darkening his face. There was no denying he was gorgeous. The sort of gorgeous that made your heart skip a beat and the breath stop in your throat for a second. The sort of gorgeous that made you think of skin against satin sheets and long kisses—and the way a man's hand felt running down across your naked flesh.

Uh-oh. No, not going to go there. If she planned to last any time at all, she was going to have to wipe that sort of thinking out of her head.

And then she noticed something that helped take it away. He was in pain. She could see him wince as he tried to move. And for just a moment, as he stood wavering against the crutches, obviously still not used to using them, she had a rush of pure empathy. Poor guy. She wanted to reach out to him, to do something to provide a little comfort, maybe some relief. If only…

"Now there's one more thing I need your help with," he was saying calmly, masking the pain with a smooth attitude. "I want to take a shower."

Okay. There it was. Jodie pressed her lips together and looked at the wall over his shoulder, holding back a volcano's worth of protest she could have spewed at him. *No emotion,* she reminded herself. *Cool and calm.*

"I really need one," he told her with a cheerfulness that seemed a little forced. "Even my hair itches. And I need a good shampoo." He wiggled his eyebrows at her. "Maybe you could rub it in for me?"

Why not a pedicure and a deep pore treatment while he was at it? There was no point in feeling sorry for the man. He just wasn't going to allow it. Gritting her teeth, she swung her gaze back to face him.

"I'd be happy to help you go soak your head," she told him carefully. "Just as long as you keep your clothes on."

His frown had a mocking edge to it. "I thought you said you weren't afraid of a little nudity."

"I can handle nudity. What I won't tolerate is familiarity. The kind your idea of shower-sharing might bring on."

Amusement played at the corners of his eyes. "So you still don't trust me."

"What was your first clue?"

"Wait a minute. Hold on here. You're lying, aren't you?"

"What?"

He shrugged as though the point was obvious. "It's yourself you don't trust. Am I right?"

She wanted to laugh, or at the very least, throw something at his handsome head. Instead, her face flushed bright red and she cursed her circulatory system.

"I knew it," he chortled, his eyelids lowering. "You're too hot-blooded to risk it. You know your naturally passionate nature will overwhelm you and you'll find yourself—"

"Heading out the door," she told him grimly, holding her head high despite the blushing. "Just watch me."

"Wait, Jodie," he said, laughing as he snagged her by the upper arm and held her from making good on her promise, despite the fact that he was tottering dangerously on the crutches. "I was only kidding. I'll be good. You'll see." He sobered, his eyes darkening as he looked down into her rebellious face. "Don't go. I really do need you."

What a delicious opening. She could laugh at him and walk away. Why not? He deserved it. And she was tempted. She could already feel the satisfaction of striding off down the walkway, leaving him stranded on his own doorstep.

Still, he halfway expected her to do that, didn't he? So why not surprise him? After all, she'd had enough training in this sort of thing to make it just possible that she might be able to keep her cool—and her distance—while performing the very task he needed her to do.

"Okay," she said, breezing past him into the house.

"I'll help you take a shower. Why not? Cleanliness is a good thing."

He turned a bit awkwardly on his crutches. "Great," he said. "I appreciate it."

She glanced down at his pajama bottoms. They were not quite as short as boxers, but the left pant leg had been split to allow it to go over the cast. The fabric was flimsy enough to leave little to the imagination, even as it pretended to cover the good parts. Despite all that expert training, her pulse stepped up a notch.

"One condition, though," she said firmly. "The pajamas stay on."

His brow furled. "That's going to make washing myself a bit difficult."

She risked looking him full in the face and found she could do it just fine. "I thought you were the sort who laughed at adversity." She smiled coolly. "Make adjustments."

"Adjustments!"

He seemed to have more to say on the subject, but she didn't stop to chat. Spotting a sliding glass door to the backyard, she made her way there and looked out. Just what she needed—a pair of plastic outdoor chairs. Sliding open the door, she grabbed them, stacked them and toted them into the house.

"Which way to the bathroom?" she asked brightly.

He still stood where she'd left him, wavering a bit on the crutches, his expression unreadable. "What are you doing?"

"Making adjustments," she told him. "The bathroom?"

He pointed the way and followed her, watching as she set up one chair inside the shower and the other just outside.

"There," she said, turning to offer a triumphant smile. "Now let's work on your leg."

It didn't take long to get him well-wrapped in plastic. She rolled the legs of the pajamas up and clipped them so that he seemed to be wearing very short shorts. And that was the rough part. Working over the cast was not a problem, but when the backs of her fingers had to brush against his warm skin, so close to forbidden areas of major interest, areas that seemed to radiate with scorching heat, she had to work very hard to keep her reactions from showing.

Kurt didn't say a word, and since she didn't look into his face, she had no idea what he was thinking. For her part, she was trying hard not to think at all.

Just get this done, she told herself. *You can scream later.*

Her background as a practicing physical therapist held her in good stead. Very quickly she had him sitting in the shower, with his left leg angled out and resting on the other chair. She tested the water and turned it on full for him, then handed him a bar of soap.

"There you go," she said with typically detached health-worker cheer. "Give me a call when you're ready to get hauled back out of there."

Turning on her heel, she left the room, then collapsed

against the wall once she was sure she was out of his sight. What a morning.

Her amusement faded as she went back over the last ten minutes and realized something. Through the whole thing, Kurt hadn't said a word to her. What was he thinking?

She frowned. He kept up a caustic front, but some-times his eyes gave him away. She really ought to pay more attention to that. She didn't trust him at all.

The first time Jodie remembered actually paying any attention to Kurt McLaughlin was when she was about fourteen and she watched him win a bull-riding contest. She'd had mixed feelings about him even then. She knew she was supposed to hate him. He was a McLaughlin—but even worse, he was beating both her brothers at something one or the other of them usually won. Matt had been away at college all year, so there was general consensus that he'd gotten a little rusty. But Rafe was at the top of his game; he'd been unofficially crowned the winner before he even came out of the chute. So it was with stunned amazement that the crowd watched as Kurt beat him out of his title, mastering the huge, red bull as though he'd been born to ride it.

She remembered the outrage she'd felt, and at the same time, the guilty surge of admiration. He'd looked so calm and in control. And her newly minted teenage hormones had tingled at his confident grin and the cool way his jeans fit him.

He'd seemed so much older then, mature and out of

reach for a girl her age. And, of course, a McLaughlin. But that image of him vanquishing his competition on the bull had stayed with her for a long time.

And now that same man was sitting next to her in her car while she steered it down the long, straight and mostly empty highway toward the vineyards. It hadn't been easy wedging in his leg, with its fiberglass cast, and maneuvering his bottom—now clothed in jersey shorts—into the seat. But finally they were rushing across the golden plain toward the low, rolling hills on the horizon.

She'd noticed that he'd popped a couple of pain pills before they left the house. There was still the suggestion of a white line around his mouth which told her that the effects of the medication hadn't kicked in yet. She winced for him, wishing she could do something to take away the obvious agony. Hopefully, the pills would work soon.

"You okay?" she asked him softly.

He didn't look up, but he nodded. "Sure," he said gruffly, and then fell silent again—proof that he really wasn't.

Her mind went back again to that hot, dusty day at the Chivaree Jamboree Rodeo. She and her best friend, Shelley, had sat in the stands, soaking up the attention from the males around them. That sort of thing had been very new to both of them at that point, and they were a little scared and very excited. She could even remember what she'd been wearing—white short shorts and a skimpy, red halter top that made her really feel like a woman for the first time ever. Watching Kurt ride that bull made her feel even more so. And when the horn blew and the clowns came out, and he'd swung down and turned to the crowd, she could have sworn he singled her out. His head went back, and a half grin curled his mouth. And she was sure he was looking right at her.

But that only lasted for seconds. Maybe she'd dreamed it. Almost immediately, a flood of Kurt's cousins had swarmed down to gather around him protectively. Everyone knew there would be a fight. There always was when McLaughlins and Allmans bumped up against each other in the claustrophobic Chivaree world of those days. And since the McLaughlin boys outnumbered the Allmans two to one, it was her brothers who usually came home with blackened eyes and split lips.

The hills coming into range snapped her out of her reverie.

"Where are we headed exactly?" she asked, glancing sideways at Kurt. "The Allman fields?"

"That's right. The ones the company owns outright."

She nodded. "How are the vineyards doing these days?"

"Not as well as we could want," he admitted. "We're still depending on crops from other suppliers for about eighty percent of the grapes."

The business had started small, just Jesse cultivating a small yield from a vineyard the Allmans had owned since the twenties. But through pure brass, her father had built it up. Now, they owned or had contracts with vineyards all over Texas hill country, and they bottled under a number of different names.

Kurt went on, talking about company business, and she was glad to see that he was feeling better. But when the facts and figures kept pouring out of him, she began to frown. Why did he seem to be so informed about all the ins and outs of her father's business dealings? For a marketing guy, he seemed awfully interested in the production numbers.

"Take the old Boca de Vaca Road turnoff up around the next bend," he told her. "We'll take it on out to Casa Azul."

That made her smile. "My father's old original vineyard?"

"Right." She could sense him studying her. "I'll bet you spent time there as a kid, didn't you?"

"Too much time." She groaned, remembering the long, fall days picking grapes when Allman Industries was just a dream her father was working toward. "Is anyone living in the old house?"

"Yes, the field manager. Who, I think, is an old friend of yours. Manny Cruz."

"Manny!" She laughed softly. Manny had been a good friend of Rafe's, and one of the few boys in town who was always ready to show up to help the Allman boys in any fight they got themselves into. "Good old Manny. It'll be great to see him again."

"He married Pam Kramer. They've got a couple of kids, from what I hear."

"Manny and Pam." She drew in a deep breath. "Wow. Time flies."

A shadow passed over her thoughts. So many old friends were married now and had children. A part of her hated that things had to change.

"Now this is what I love," Kurt said suddenly, startling her. "Look out there. Can you find a sky like that anywhere else? Can you see as far? Does anywhere else look this golden?" He turned to smile at her, pushing his Stetson back on his head. "That's why I came back. Texas is home."

She felt the same way, only she hadn't ever lived in any other state. But she knew what he meant. Texas was a place where there was room to breathe. Good thing, too, because once she took in that smile, the one thing she needed was more air.

They wound their way into the hills, and suddenly, vineyards covered the landscape, each vine newly leafed out and flowing with graceful promise.

"These through here belong to the Newcombs," Kurt told her. "And just up there past that stand of cottonwoods, the Allman property begins."

Fascinating. Ownership of this acreage had expanded a lot since the days when she and her brothers and sister had been forced to work the harvest. But once again she had to wonder why Kurt was taking such an active interest in these things that would seem to be beyond his need to know.

"Go slow through here," he said, pulling out his camera. "I want to take a few shots."

"Do you want me to stop?"

"Not yet. I'll tell you when."

He leaned out the open window as best he could, being tethered by his cast, taking one shot after another as she slowed.

"You said you were working on an idea for an ad campaign?" she asked.

"Right," he said shortly.

She waited a moment, but he didn't volunteer any more information. She frowned, looking out at the perfectly ordinary rows of grapevines he was taking pictures of, wondering what he could possibly have in mind. Whatever it was, he didn't seem to want to share.

"Pull down this dirt road," he said at last. "Let's go back in and stop. I want to get a closer look at these vines."

She did as he ordered, then pulled over and turned off the engine. "Are you sure you want to do this?" she asked, thinking of the trouble they'd had getting him into the car. "I don't know how often you're going to want to drag that cast in and out of this cramped space."

"I'm okay," he told her. "There's something I really need to see here."

She helped him out, and he did much better than he had before. He was starting to get the hang of it. Either that, or his mind was so thoroughly involved with whatever it was he was investigating, he had forgotten the pain.

The crutches sank into the rich loam, but he didn't

seem to notice. She followed behind, glad she'd worn slacks today, but trying to avoid getting sand in her shoes.

"This is really an impressive sight, isn't it?" he said. "Row upon row of these brave little soldiers."

Gee, that was almost poetry. He'd said the last softly, as though he didn't really mean for her to hear. She looked at him, wondering what went on inside that handsome head. Whatever it was, she wished there was a better way to get a hint of it.

Starting off, he led her to a vine that didn't look quite as healthy as the others. Leaning on one crutch, he reached out and plucked a few leaves, studying them intently.

"You see that?" he said, holding out one leaf.

She stared, biting her lip. "It looks okay to me."

He shook his head. "No. Something is definitely wrong. And look at those." He gestured toward a row of vines. "The vines just aren't bearing the way they should be. We've got to figure out what's going on here."

She watched him, surprised he was so absorbed in this. It hardly seemed to be something a marketing guy would want to immerse himself in.

"Listen," she said. "Why don't you leave this to the growers to worry about? Or have Manny call out the Department of Agriculture. I thought we came out here to take pictures."

"We did." He frowned. "Do me a favor," he said. "Pick a few more leaves, just randomly, but keep them separate. I want to take them back and get some opinions."

"Keep them separate?" She gazed at him, bewildered. "How am I supposed to do that?"

"You've got pockets, don't you?"

"Pockets," she muttered, but she began to do as he'd asked. She had three pockets in her dark blue slacks and two in the light, checkered shirt she wore. Once she'd stuffed each of them full, she began to feel like a pack animal.

The sound of a vehicle, traveling fast, distracted her. "Oh, look. Someone's coming."

A bright red pickup truck was barreling along an access road toward where they stood among the vines. They both stopped and looked up. Jodie frowned. There was something menacing about the way the truck was hurtling toward them—something she didn't like. She began to edge closer to where Kurt was standing, instinctively looking to him for protection.

Suddenly, the unmistakable sound of gunfire split the air.

Chapter Four

"What the hell?"

The words tore out of Kurt as he grabbed Jodie, pushed her down into the dirt and threw himself on top of her. His hat flew off, and the cast fell heavily against her leg, but she hardly noticed. The rest of his body was pressing her into the earth, and she had a weird sensation of drowning.

"Lie still," he barked at her. "That damned idiot."

"Who?" she tried to ask, struggling for breath. "What's going on?"

The pickup came to a gravel-crunching stop very near them. She could hear the cab door open, but she couldn't raise her head enough to look up and see what was happening. The smell and taste of dirt filled her nose and mouth.

"McLaughlin!" The shout came from the pickup. "Get off this land."

Kurt swore softly and raised his upper body. "Manny, are you crazy?" he shouted back. "You trying to kill somebody?"

"I only wish." Jodie heard a sound of disgust coming from the man in the truck. "Don't worry, McLaughlin. I didn't aim nowhere near you. This time."

The sound of a shotgun being cocked hit Jodie like a clap of thunder.

"But I could. Like I told you before, get back in your car and get your damned McLaughlin butt off this land. This here is Allman property and—"

"Manny Cruz."

Kurt had moved enough to let Jodie wiggle her way out from under him. She pushed up into a sitting position. "Manny, this is one heck of a way to welcome me home. You're as crazy as you ever were, aren't you?"

"Jodie?" Manny stared for a moment, then a wide grin broke out on his dark, handsome face. "Hey, Jodie! I haven't seen you since…since…"

"For a long time," she said, helping him out. She rose shakily to her feet and waved at him. "So, how've you been?"

"Hey, great." He looked pleased as punch. "Did you know Pam Kramer and I got hitched?"

"I heard."

"And we've got two kids. You got to come out to the house and see them."

Jodie swallowed and managed a smile, wiping her face with her sleeve. "I'd love to. You won't shoot us, will you?"

Manny looked shocked. He glanced at the shotgun still resting in his hands and quickly put it down against the truck as though he had no further use for it.

"Hell, no. That was just a warning for this McLaughlin punk." His face changed along with his tone of voice. "Hey, what are you doing with this guy, anyway?"

"That's a question I've asked myself a few times today," she told him, giving Kurt a sideways glance. "Dad hired him, though, so I guess you'd better not shoot him."

Manny shook his head. "I'd heard that, but I didn't want to believe it." His tone conveyed his deep distaste. "McLaughlins don't work for Allmans. Or the other way round, either. It just ain't natural."

"I'll tell you what ain't natural," Kurt countered, starting toward the man, his voice hard with anger. "It ain't natural or legal or right for you to shoot at people. If you've got a problem with me, let's take care of it right now."

Both men bristled with belligerence, but then Manny's face changed as he took in the cast on Kurt's leg. Kurt seemed to have forgotten about it. He was rushing toward Manny, even though he'd lost his crutches, hopping on his good foot, his anger giving him the strength to make the charge. Manny looked confused. How was he going to fight a man with a broken leg?

Suddenly, Jodie began to laugh.

"This isn't funny," Kurt said, pausing to glare back at her.

"Oh, yes it is," she said, laughing harder. "This is the funniest thing I ever saw. Us hitting the dirt, and Manny driving up in his truck, and you trying to fight him with only one good leg." She sank back down to sit on the ground, and laughed until her sides hurt.

The two men stood glaring at her, both with hands balled into fists at their sides. But the need to fight seemed to have evaporated, at least for now. And for that, she was grateful.

The old sky-blue farmhouse didn't look quite the way it had when Jodie and her family had come out here years before. A small, pink oleander bush stood next to the porch, petunias brightened a window box, and the roof looked new. A cute little pond shimmered in the sunlight where there once had been a mud hole from a leaky faucet. Jodie pulled the car up beside the driveway and came around to help Kurt. Manny had sent them on ahead while he went to take a few workers to another field.

Meanwhile, Kurt was telling her about his last visit to the vineyards a few weeks before.

"I didn't see Manny, but some of his workers followed me everywhere I went. They stayed just out of reach, but communicated with their boss on walkie-talkies, letting him know what I was doing."

She'd been moving his bad leg out of the car, but now she stopped to look him in the face. "What *were* you doing?"

His smile was guileless. "Looking things over."

She gave him a penetrating look. There was no point in hiding the fact that she had her suspicions about him. "I see."

But he seemed oblivious. "And the next day there was a message left on my desk. Something about McLaughlins staying off Allman land."

"Or what?" she said, handing him his crutches as he made his way onto his feet.

He shrugged. "There were a few nasty suggestions as to what might happen to me, but I won't bore you with the details."

She nodded. "So you decided to trot right back out here and give him the old nah-nah-nah-nah, huh?"

"Of course." He looked bemused that she would expect anything else. "He had no right to try to keep me away."

She spread out her hands as though explaining to the heavens. "Of course."

As they started up the walkway, a small child came rocketing out the front door. His lower lip stuck out with stark determination, the tyke was heading away as fast as his chubby little legs would take him. From inside the house, a voice came sailing after him.

"Lenny, you get back here! Don't you dare go down there by that pond!"

Kurt handed Jodie one of his crutches and took a side

step to intercept the little fellow, scooping him up and dangling him at eye level.

"Hi," Kurt said to the child, whose mouth was hanging open in astonishment. "Where you goin' so fast?"

The little boy struggled for a moment, but Kurt's wide grin seemed to mesmerize him, and soon he was grinning back.

"Oh, my, how did you catch him?" A pretty, young woman with bright red hair appeared in the doorway, a baby on her hip. "Thanks so much. He keeps running down to the pond and jumping right in, and then I have to wash the frog's eggs out of his hair."

"I've got one about this age myself," Kurt told her pleasantly, carrying the little one toward the house. "I know what they're like."

Jodie would have marveled at how well he was learning to maneuver with his crutches—or without them—but her attention was riveted on the children. She usually tried to avoid being around kids this young. Even after all these years, it still hurt so much. Turning away from babies the way some turned away from the sight of blood, she tried to focus on her old friend instead.

"Pam?" she said, waiting for the young woman to turn her gaze in her direction.

The woman gasped. "No way! Jodie! Jodie Allman! I heard you were back. It's been years!"

Jodie exchanged hugs with Pam, carefully avoiding the baby she still held to her body. Pam chattered happily, escorting them into her house as though she'd been expecting them.

"You're just in time for lunch. Come on in. I'll put another couple of plates on the table."

"Oh, we couldn't impose."

"Are you kidding? I always cook enough for all the hands, and I just got word that somebody's girlfriend made a run into town and showed up with a big sack of Mickey D's, so I was going to have good food going to waste. You'll be doing me a favor. Come on in and sit down. It'll be ready in no time at all. Where's Manny? Has he seen you yet? He's going to be thrilled! All he ever talks about is the old days and how much fun it was fighting McLaughlins."

She cast a covert glance at Kurt. "I guess you're one of them, though, ain't you? I seem to remember you." She rolled her eyes as though anyone could see that was a joke. Remember Kurt? Who could forget? "Jodie and I were in class with your sister, Tracy, until she left to go to that private boarding school." She gave Jodie a significant look. "Remember that? I don't know if we were more jealous or outraged at the time. But it sure did cause a stir. Boarding school, of all things!"

"A lot of people go to boarding school," Kurt protested.

"Not around here they don't."

Jodie made formal introductions and explained that they had seen Manny out in the fields. While Pam kept up a running monologue, she got the table set, food served, Lenny into a high chair and the baby into a little recliner. Jodie was in awe.

"Pam," she said at last. "I remember when you couldn't get your Latin homework done because you had to paint your toenails one night. Now you're multitasking. What happened?"

Pam shook back her red curls and laughed. "I grew up, Jodie. Surely you did, too."

Had she? Jodie wasn't so sure.

"Having kids really changes you, you know? It starts when you're pregnant. You just become a different person when you start thinking about the life you're creating."

Pam turned to look into Jodie's face. "But maybe you do know. For all I know, you've been married and had a dozen kids by now." She grinned at her old friend. "Or at least one. You've got that look. How about it, honey? Do you have any kids?"

Jodie's mouth was dry and her heart pounded in her chest. This was just so stupid. Pam hadn't meant anything; she was just being friendly. There was no way she could have known about the baby Jodie had lost all those years ago.

Hopefully, no one in Chivaree knew.

Luckily she didn't have to answer, because Pam's youngest started to fuss, and Kurt picked her up to comfort her in the most natural way possible. Jodie envied him his ease with little ones. If she could just get control of herself, maybe she could get to be that comfortable. It was way past time for her to work on it. More and more of her old friends were going to be thrusting their children at her. She couldn't keep acting like a vampire seeing the sun. It was ridiculous.

Still, she moved across the room and started helping Pam, just to make sure Kurt didn't try to get her to hold the baby, as well.

And then Manny appeared in the doorway, taking off his straw hat and scowling just as darkly as he had out in the vineyard when he saw Kurt holding his child.

"Here," he said gruffly, reaching for her.

Pam took in the tension in a glance and began chattering again, getting everyone to sit down at the table and taking the baby back to the bedroom to put her into her crib. Manny and Kurt stared at each other until Pam called Kurt to come back to the baby's room to see the new train set she'd ordered for Lenny, thinking he'd be interested because of his own little one.

Once Kurt was out of the room, Manny looked Jodie in the eye, shaking his head.

"Will you explain to me what your dad is doing hirin' this bum?" he said in a low voice, his dark eyes flashing. "You can tell he's up to no good."

Jodie felt jolted. Finally someone agreed with her. She looked eagerly into his gaze. "You feel it, too?"

"Sure." He shrugged as though he thought it was a no-brainer. "He's a McLaughlin, ain't he?"

She frowned. It was more than that. Was this just a knee-jerk reaction Manny had? For that matter, were her own feelings about Kurt just as blind?

"Well, my brothers seem to think he's doing a good job," she pointed out, wanting to be fair.

Manny grunted. "Around here, we don't call a man a cowboy 'til we seen him ride."

Pam and Kurt came back and sat down to eat. Manny brought out a handful of glasses and a bottle of Allman Vineyards Chardonnay.

"You'll like this one," he said, giving them a little background on the vintage as he began to pour out the golden liquid into each glass. "It's fruity, but so light you'd almost swear it had some natural carbonation to it."

Jodie smiled. She could remember when Manny was a guy who spent most of his free time working on cars, and now here he was, a wine connoisseur. She watched as Kurt put his hand over his glass.

"None for me, thanks," he said.

Manny's face darkened. He'd obviously decided to take that as an insult. Jodie winced, then realized Kurt was turning down the alcohol because of the pain pills he'd taken. But the conversation had moved on, and it was too late to tell Manny that.

Jodie and Pam did most of the talking during the meal, dredging up old times and laughing over old incidents. Manny and Kurt were mostly silent. Now and then, Jodie looked over at Kurt, wishing he would join in on the conversation. But finally she realized he was thinking about something and not really listening to the chattering.

Manny's thoughts were written on his face. He detested Kurt. But she was pretty sure Kurt wasn't thinking about Manny at all. He had something else on his mind and he was giving her no hints as to what it was.

Jodie helped clear away the dishes, and Manny went to hold Lenny while Pam cut them each a sliver of rich lemon cake for dessert. Kurt didn't look up when Jodie placed his piece in front of him, and she was about to give him a kick under the table when he suddenly pulled out a handful of the leaves he'd taken from the grapevines and began to arrange them on the tabletop.

"What the hell are you doin'?" Manny demanded.

Kurt looked up as though he was surprised to see anyone else there. "I've been thinking. Listen, about the problem with the vines…"

"We had the guy from the Department of Agriculture out here three times," Manny told him dismissively. "If he can't figure out what's wrong, what makes you think you can?"

"I'm no expert, but—"

Manny snorted. "Damn right. You're a McLaughlin, ain't ya? Ever done anything right?"

Jodie looked quickly at Kurt. In the old days, those would have been fighting words. She could already picture the two men rolling around on the linoleum floor, trading insults and punches in the old traditional dance of hatred between the two sides. She fully expected to see Kurt's face flush and his eyes gleam with anger. Instead, he seemed more impatient with the nonsense Manny was spewing than anything.

"Listen, this is important. There's something about these leaves that keeps reminding me of something, and I'm not sure what it is. But I did my undergraduate work in botany at the university, and I still have ties to some professors there. I'm going to send them these leaves and see if they can come up with anything."

Manny's face didn't change, but he dropped the antagonistic insults. "I don't suppose they'll come up with anything new," he said, as he watched Kurt's face.

"You never know. They are developing new ways to diagnose this stuff all the time. If anyone knows the latest, my old professor Willard Charlton will have the scoop. He loves keeping up with the cutting-edge research."

Manny still looked suspicious, but what Kurt had said had definitely engaged his interest.

"What do you think it is?" he asked.

"I don't know. But look here on the back of the leaves. There are little clusters of tiny shot holes. You see?" He held the leaves up to the light so Manny could see them. "You really have to look close to notice them. I'm thinking some sort of new fungus or parasite is attacking the plants, something so small, we don't detect it easily."

Manny took one of the leaves and stared at it, looking from one way and then another. "We've tried fungicides," he said gruffly. "And I spray all the time. If it was a parasite…"

"If it was anything we could recognize, we'd know it by now."

Kurt asked Jodie for the leaves he'd had her set aside, and put them out in a line across from the infected leaves. He went on talking, showing things to Manny, and Jodie watched as the vineyard manager's belligerence died, and reluctant respect took over. Soon they were talking together like regular acquaintances, if not actual friends.

And just like that he was winning over Manny. Jodie shook her head with a tinge of resentment. She couldn't believe it. This was always happening around the man!

"How come you go out of your way to charm everybody except for me?" Jodie asked Kurt later, as they were driving home.

"You?" Obviously surprised by her comment, he grinned at her. "I know you're too smart for me, Jodie. I wouldn't insult you by trying to charm you."

Watching the road, she waved at the driver of a long cow trailer as she passed him. She couldn't help nursing feelings just this side of being hurt. Which was ridiculous, of course. Still, she was only human.

"Somehow you manage to get everyone else on your side. It's like you have this fine sense of exactly what will bring them around, and you play your cards just right. But all you do is needle me." She glanced over at where he sat. Oh, lord, she was whining, wasn't she? "So tell me why."

He sighed and leaned back. He didn't say anything for a long moment, and she began to think he was going to ignore her question. Finally, he responded.

"I can't tell you that, Miss Jodie Allman," he drawled in his best Texas accent. "With you, I'm just doin' what comes naturally, I guess."

"So you have a natural antagonism for me," she ventured.

"Could be."

Oh, he wasn't even trying! A flash of anger shot through her. "Either that," she snapped, "or your natural state is pretty Neanderthal."

"Hey, that hurts. I consider myself a real gentleman."

Okay, he was teasing. No need for her to take anything he said seriously.

"Of the old school," she shot back. "Circa 1210 in Outer Mongolia."

He chuckled. The way he was sitting, she could tell that he was completely relaxed. Well, that was one thing anyway. At least he didn't hate her so much that she made him tense up.

He'd taken more pain medication before they'd left Manny and Pam's ranch house. By the time they had walked out the door and piled back into the car, he and Manny had been exchanging e-mail addresses, and Pam had been planning to set up play dates for her little Lenny and Kurt's Katy.

It was infuriating how he seemed to stay in control of every situation all the time. She was going to do her best to find some way to get under his skin. It would be interesting to see him lose that finely honed sense of command.

"I was just remembering the first time I really knew you existed," he said all at once, out of the blue.

"At the Chivaree rodeo?" she asked before she could stop herself. A vision of how he'd looked as he triumphantly swung down off that bull and seemed to catch her eye in the stands flashed back like a delicious shock of sensation. But she immediately regretted saying anything and bit her tongue.

"The rodeo?" He frowned as though he had no idea what she was talking about, then shook his head.

She groaned inside, knowing she'd been a little too obvious. But maybe he hadn't noticed.

"No, not that. It was when we were both pretty young."

Even though she wasn't looking at him, she could feel him studying her profile as she drove. Her cheeks began to heat up, and she cursed silently. She wasn't usually self-conscious with men. Why did she keep doing this whenever Kurt paid a little too much attention to her?

"Do you remember," he said softly, "the time my sister had a birthday party at Sam Houston Park, and you were hanging around on the outskirts, watching it?" There was a warm hint of amusement in his voice. "I think I was twelve, so you must have been about seven or eight."

She frowned. That was a bit early for major recollections. She tried to think.

"I saw you watching the proceedings like a waif with

her nose pressed to the glass. I thought you were a cute little thing, so I decided to get you to join in. I went down by the merry-go-round, where you were lurking, and I invited you to come on up. But you scowled at me and shook your head."

He laughed aloud. "You still have that look a lot today—that look that says, 'Don't tempt me. I won't be compromised!'"

She wasn't about to dignify his silliness with a response, so she pressed her lips together.

"Anyway, I went back up and got you an ice-cream cone and brought it down to you. Looking back, it was like offering a piece of meat to a wolf puppy—holding it there, talking soothingly to you, watching you come warily forward to get the cone. Like a little wild child." He paused, remembering. "When you think about it, you Allman kids often seemed like little beasts in those days."

"Oh, for heaven's sake!" She'd had about enough of this. She didn't want to hear it, didn't want to think of how it had been back then. "We did not. Things like that were all in your head, and you McLaughlins spent so much time spreading that nonsense, it was like a giant propaganda campaign. You were the ones who started calling us the Allman Gang. We knew you were doing it, and we resented it!"

"I held the cone out," he went on as though she hadn't spoken. "You came closer and closer, your eyes glued to that ice cream. Oh, you wanted it, all right. And finally, you took it from my hand and looked up at me and almost smiled."

"Almost?"

He nodded. "Almost."

She waited for him to go on, and fleeting memories of the birthday flooded through her. She recalled skulking around the edges of the festivities, feeling like an outcast, wishing she would be invited in.

"You took that cone and you were getting ready to taste it. I was getting ready to enjoy you tasting it. And then you looked up, and suddenly, everything changed. You yelled a name at me, threw the cone down in the dirt, turned on your heel and took off, racing across the park with your pigtails flying." He looked at her as though that reaction still puzzled him. "Do you remember that?"

She tried. She remembered parts, but only vaguely. And she surely didn't remember throwing the ice cream cone in the dirt. Actually, knowing the way she'd felt about ice cream as a kid, she found that part a bit hard to believe.

But now that he'd mentioned it, she could remember a boy standing there holding the cone, looking at her. Yes, the picture became clearer. Was that really Kurt? She didn't think she could have named him at the time. She could remember feeling embarrassed and gratified all at once. And she thought she recalled a sense of guilt. What was that for?

"My young male ego was very affronted at what you

did," he told her lightly. "I guess that's why I still have it in my mind after all these years."

She thought about that for a long moment, then shook her head. "How do you know it was me?"

"I knew you were an Allman. That was obvious. And I asked my sister who you were."

Jodie frowned. "Tracy was watching all this?"

He shrugged. "She was around. It was her birthday party."

Wait. Yes, she remembered now. She could see the cone lying in the dirt, ice cream flying from it. She must have thrown it down, just as he'd said. But why?

"Looks like we're almost home," Kurt said. "Why don't you just drop me at the curb and go on in to the office to see if anything needs my attention. You can call me from there if anything does." He winced, moving his leg. "But make sure it's important. It's almost quitting time."

"Fine," she said, her voice a little strained, as she pulled in front of his house. Turning off the engine, she started to get out to help him, but he stopped her.

"I can get it," he said. "You just go on."

"Okay," she said reluctantly. "I guess I'll see you tomorrow."

"That's the plan," he said, reaching for the door handle.

"Kurt, wait." She was nuts. Completely nuts. He was going to see that she was desperately trying to think of reasons to delay him getting out of the car.

And why was she doing that? Oh, yeah. It was because she was nuts.

"Uh… how does your leg feel?" she asked quickly.

"Not too bad."

"You were much too hard on it today," she fretted. "I hope it hasn't set back your recovery."

One eyebrow rose sardonically. "Are you actually concerned about my welfare?"

"Of course I am."

"Ah. Just as one human being to another, no doubt."

"No." She was being an idiot, but she couldn't stop herself. "Kurt, I…" She winced and looked away, biting her lip. "I do care. Actually, I…I kind of like you. Whenever I can forget the McLaughlin part of you," she added hastily.

He laughed gruffly, and she looked up in time to see him reach out and touch her cheek, his fingers leaving a trail of sweet sensation.

"I'm so tempted to kiss you right now," he said softly, his eyes glowing. "If you weren't an Allman, I might actually do it."

This was all wrong and exactly what she'd been so determined to guard against. So why did she find herself smiling at him and feeling kind of shy? And why was her heart thumping in her chest like a wild thing? She was actually leaning toward him as though she was being pulled by some irresistible force.

And he was leaning toward her.

She closed her eyes and his lips touched hers. Just barely. The gesture was quick, almost casual, like the salute of a friend rather than a lover, but it made its mark. A wave of warm pleasure surged through her as the full, male essence of him swept over her—his wide shoulders, warm, masculine scent and smooth, tanned skin. All of this filled her with a deep yearning and she sighed as he pulled away again.

Her eyes flew open in horror. Had he noticed the sigh? She saw quick surprise flash in his gaze, and then a half smile before he leaned toward her again. This time the gentle touch was gone and she tasted raw male desire that made her heart stop.

But once again he drew back so quickly that she was left off balance, blinking up at him with her lips parted. He hesitated, his gaze caressing her mouth for just a moment before he began pulling himself out of the car. At first it was a bit awkward for him, and she had to stifle the urge to help. But once he got his bearings, he seemed to be fine. She watched as he made his way up the walkway toward his front door. He didn't even look back.

And why did that bring something that felt almost like a lump to her throat? She wanted him to turn, didn't she? She wanted him to smile at her, give her a wink, maybe—something personal. Let her know that he was going to miss her while they were apart. Let her know that he had enjoyed her company for the day and was looking forward to seeing her tomorrow. Maybe even let her know that he didn't regret the kiss.

Because the truth was, that was how she was feeling.

Yup, the verdict was in. She was nuts.

Chapter Five

"I am not helping you take another shower."

Jodie was at Kurt's door again, and he was dressed the same way he had been the morning before—in almost nothing. But this time, his hair was wet and he had a towel hanging over his shoulders. So when he said, "I already took care of that," she believed him and felt a distinct sense of relief.

Still, she had a feeling he'd remained at this level of undress just to provoke her. Today she vowed to be unprovokeable.

She'd spent a sleepless night worrying about the kiss. And then she'd had her morning cup of coffee, looked at herself in the mirror and wondered what all the anguish had been about. As a kiss, it had been pretty quick and uneventful. Nothing to get herself in a dither about.

And she almost had herself convinced—until she'd remembered how she'd practically gone into a swoon and had let out that sigh full of longing. What would she have done if he'd actually taken her into his arms? She had a sinking feeling that she would have gotten swept away by the moment.

Oh, well. Good thing she recognized the danger signals. That should help her keep her guard up from now on. And as she made herself meet his gaze with a cool look, she was glad to see he didn't seem to be anxious to bring up the kiss himself.

"Good," she said briskly, coming right in and dropping a stack of manila folders on the table. "Now all we have to do is get some decent clothes on you."

He turned on his crutches, following her progress through his house. "What is this annoying obsession you have with hiding human body parts?" he teased.

"It's *my* obsession, and I'm standing by it," she retorted.

No, indeed, he wasn't going to get her goat today. She glanced down the hall toward his bedroom. She'd already raided it the day before, getting him ready for the trip to the vineyards, so she would feel right at home visiting it again. The only trouble was, the way he was standing was right in the path she had to take.

She gazed at him challengingly. "Make way. I'm going to get you dressed."

He didn't move, and one eyebrow rose quizzically.

"You wouldn't take advantage of a man on crutches, would you?"

"Heavens, no." She smiled at him, her chin high. "I'd knock him off them first."

He nodded, grinning. "Of that I have no doubt."

But he shuffled out of her way, and she went into his room and came back with sweatpants and a polo shirt.

"You really are going to have to work harder on maintaining a businesslike appearance, you know," she scolded. "Otherwise, people are going to get the wrong idea about what is going on here."

"What *is* going on here?" he asked, as she handed him the shirt. He dropped one crutch and began fumbling with the opening until she sighed and reached out to help him. "Is there any hope it might turn into something interesting?"

"That depends on your definition of interesting," she said, as she pulled his shirt over his head. Her fingers lingered on his skin, and she was glad his face was under cloth so he couldn't see her reaction. Her eyes closed for just a moment as she soaked in the pure maleness of him. "I very much doubt we would have definitions that agreed," she added a bit breathlessly.

"You might be right." He scrunched into the shirt and, as his head cleared the opening, she found herself staring right into his eyes. Suddenly, his free hand was sliding into the hair at the back of her head, and somehow he managed to pull her close enough so that her body was touching his in all the wrong places.

"For instance, I'd say this qualifies," he said, his voice rough in a deep way that seemed to resonate inside her.

She stared back into his gaze, her heart in her throat. If he knew how much she liked this, she would be in big trouble. Best to pretend it was no big deal. But how did she do that when every fiber of her being wanted to feel him tight and hard against her? Still, it had to be done. Gathering her strength, she pulled away from him.

True to form, he laughed. *You see?* his laughter said. *I'm just kidding around. This is no big deal.*

She bit her lip, wishing she didn't feel this overwhelming attraction to the man. What was she going to do to stop from melting into another kiss with him? Too much of this and she was going to surrender.

"Hey, don't look so sad," he teased. "I can take the shirt back off."

She reacted instinctively, reaching out to give him a whack in the shoulder, and he caught her hand, pulling her close again.

"This could be considered sexual harassment," she said stoutly, firmly determined not to let herself notice how good he smelled, all freshly showered and clean and smooth…

He raised one dark eyebrow. "What are you going to do? Turn me in to the big boss?"

"Why not? You deserve it." She licked her dry lips. "And he is my father. He'll do whatever I ask, don't you think?"

Kurt laughed again, looking quizzical. "In a word, no." But he let her go.

"That's the problem," she said, straightening her cotton shirt and managing to keep her cool, though her senses were reeling. "I need more clout so you'll listen to my threats."

He noticed she was still holding the sweatpants and looking doubtful, and he took them from her. "Don't worry. I'll sit down and put these on myself."

She almost thanked him, but she stopped herself in time. That would be pathetic, wouldn't it?

Things had changed a lot between them in the last two days. She still didn't trust him, but she had to admit, she was starting to enjoy being with him. Oh, danger, danger! She was going to have to toughen her defenses here. Hadn't she been down this road with a McLaughlin before?

And that was from where she would draw her strength. All she had to do was remember how his cousin Jeremy had abandoned her when she'd needed him most. That ought to keep her from letting another McLaughlin get into her heart.

The toys were driving her crazy.

Ignore them. Pretend they're rocks. Keep your head down and work.

But no matter what she was doing, she could see them out of the corner of her eye. Fuzzy little stuffed animals, a pink stuffed horse, two dolls with purple hair, a silver ball, a tall, skinny monster with green scales. They were crowding out everything else with the essence of *baby*. This was not how she wanted to waste her day.

She and Kurt had spent two hours working on his plan for a new ad campaign. They'd spent half the time brainstorming, and now were high-grading the results and blocking out a proposal. Once they had this down cold, it would go to the ad agency Allman Industries worked with, and the agency would come back with its own ideas.

And truth be told—they worked well together. Kurt was definitely in charge, but he listened to her without condescension and often took her advice to heart. She felt like a respected member of a team rather than hired help.

The phone rang, and Kurt hobbled into the hall to take the call. Jodie saw her chance and rose from the table, scooping up the toys, one after another, dumping them onto a corner of the couch. Now, to cover them with something. Gazing about the room, she didn't see anything better than one of the big, flat pillows from the couch itself, and she picked one up for the purpose.

Kurt came back into the room just as she was placing the pillow. She flushed when she realized he'd seen her. She put it down with relish, like a wicked stepmother out to smother the poor little toys. She turned, knowing she looked guilty. He frowned, looking puzzled, but he didn't ask for an explanation.

"That was Pam," he said. "She's going to bring

Lenny over to play with Katy on Saturday when they come into town to do some shopping."

"Saturday? Oh. Great." She couldn't keep the relief out of her voice. "I won't be here."

He frowned, looking back at the couch, where the toys were peeking out from under the pillow like forlorn refugees.

"Why do you hate children?" he asked.

The word *hate* made her cringe. "I don't hate children," she protested.

"I saw how you were yesterday at Lenny and Pam's. You would have thought the kids had something you were afraid you might catch."

So he'd noticed that.

"Oh, please." She sat back down at the table and shuffled some papers. "I've never been around kids much. So I'm just not comfortable interacting with them." She risked a look at his face. He was still frowning. "They just don't figure in my life, that's all."

"How tragic for you."

"Not at all," she said defensively. "I like it that way."

He sat down across from her, looking concerned. "You don't want to ever have children?"

She shook her head, dismissing his concerns. "It just works out that way for some people, you know."

She knew it was silly to have this anxiety about kids, but she couldn't help it. Why couldn't people respect that and leave her alone?

Once people had children, they seemed to think that

everyone else should want to drool over them all day, too. So far, she'd been lucky to avoid Kurt's baby, but she had no doubt her luck couldn't hold forever. She had plans made, excuses to use, just in case anyone tried to get her to do anything with the baby. It wasn't that she couldn't handle holding a little one like that. She just didn't want to.

Kurt seemed to have given up on scrutinizing her mind-set and gone back to his own problems.

"I'm afraid I'm going to have some trouble where Katy is concerned," he said, absently playing with his pencil. "My sister has been taking care of her most days, along with my mother. And Tracy is talking about leaving town very soon."

"Oh?"

He nodded and grimaced. "Tracy thinks she's found the love of her life," he said wryly.

"Maybe she has."

"Maybe. But since this is perfect lover number—oh, I don't know, about four hundred and fifty—I'd say the odds are against it." His smile was sad and fleeting. "Talk about someone who never gives up hope. A real optimist is our Tracy. She's already got two divorces under her belt. Looks like she's aiming for number three."

"You know, you're being much too cynical." She couldn't believe she was actually defending his sister after the cruel way she'd taunted Jodie when they were kids. Maybe it was the feminine right to change her mind she was standing up for. "She may really have found the right one this time."

His sexy mouth tilted in a smile. "You mean, as in 'Even a stopped clock is right twice a day'?"

"That wasn't exactly what I meant, but it will do."

He shook his head. "I might have more hope if she would start looking for a mate in places where nice guys hang out. Instead, she picks the scene that caters to jerks."

"Bars and pool halls?" Jodie asked sympathetically.

He glanced up, his gaze guileless. "No. The law firm where she works."

"Kurt!"

"I'm not kidding. Every man she brings home wants to be my legal and financial advisor and, in the course of conversation, it usually turns out he's got some great business idea that is a sure thing and he only needs a small business loan to get it off the ground."

She made a face. "Scam artists?"

"To one degree or another. Dreamers, too. They're as optimistic as she is."

She studied his face. He was frustrated with his sister's bad judgment, but worried about her, as well. That much was surely evident. And from what she remembered of Tracy, worrying was probably justified.

"It's good to dream," she said softly, holding out hope.

"Sure. As long as you do something to back it up. Dreams aren't much use without some muscle behind them."

He went on, but she was only listening lightly. She'd recalled something during the night, lying in her bed and staring at the ceiling. The whole scene where Kurt—only she hadn't realized it was him at the time—had handed her the ice cream cone and she'd thrown it in the dirt had come to her while she was dozing. She remembered what had made her throw his generous gesture back at him.

She'd reached out, and the cone was in her hand. Anticipation trembled in her. The Allmans were dirt poor in those days, and ice cream cones didn't grow on trees. She'd looked up at the boy—Kurt—to say "thank you," as her mama had taught her to do. But what she'd seen behind Kurt had changed everything.

There was Tracy, along with a few of her friends, all laughing and making faces at Jodie. It suddenly became very clear that she was in the position of the poor, little beggar girl, and they were mocking her for it. She hadn't been invited to the party and they knew it. Even at seven years of age, Jodie had learned the hard way that pride was sometimes more important to the psyche than shame, even if it cost her the thing she wanted most. That was the Allman way. So she'd thrown the cone in the mud and run off, tears making trails through the dirt on her little-girl face. But they were tears that Tracy and her friends would never see.

Should she tell Kurt about it?

Maybe. Someday. Not now.

He'd been the only one to acquit himself in the incident. Gazing at him now, that gave her a glow. He was actually a pretty good person. And that was rare for a McLaughlin.

Still, there was this odd situation with him working for the Allmans. She just couldn't reconcile that with the antagonisms of the past. What had made him do it?

Kurt chose that moment to bring up the new production numbers, and that gave Jodie the opening she needed to do a little digging.

"Tell me why you're so interested in everything that has to do with Allman Industries," she said, leaning across the table and studying his reaction.

He gazed at her levelly, totally aware of why she was asking.

"I work there," he said simply.

She narrowed her gaze, pinning him to the wall—or, at least, trying to. "You don't seem to treat your job like an everyday worker would. You seem much too involved in what's going on behind the scenes."

"Behind the scenes?" He used a mockingly dramatic voice. "Are you sniffing out a conspiracy here?"

"All I know is," she said, jabbing at him with a finger, "you fit the picture of someone who is thinking about trying to take over the company."

He looked Cheshire-cat smug. "Do I?"

He didn't deny it! What did that mean? How arrogant!

"Is that your plan? Is that *it?*"

She was beginning to think it actually might be true. Glaring at him, she went on. "Is this just another chapter in the same old feud? I know you'll deny it, but why else would you come to work for my father? You were raised to hate us." She shook her head. "It seems like the only logical explanation."

He watched her as though bemused. "Wow. Once you get rolling, you forget all about the brakes, don't you?" he said.

"Kurt—"

He held up a hand. "My turn. Jodie, I will tell you exactly why I signed on at Allman Industries."

She took a deep breath and nodded. "Okay. Go ahead."

"It was the best job I could find."

She waited, but there didn't seem to be any more information coming.

"That's it?" she asked in disbelief.

"That's it." He seemed to enjoy her consternation, but finally he relented and told her more.

"I worked in management at a major multinational corporation in New York for a few years and did pretty well. Made a good salary. When I came back to Chivaree, I knew I was going to be taking a pay cut no matter what I did. But when I found out the only openings were at Pete's garage and the busboy position at Millie's café, I decided I had to get creative. Allman Industries was the only large and thriving business in town. So I went to see your father."

Despite herself, she was impressed—if he was really on the level with her. Could she believe him?

The only alternative was to go on thinking he was somehow working to undermine her father's business. And when you came right down to it, that was beginning to look a little silly, even to her. Why would he bother? She was starting to think his innocent act was pretty convincing. Everyone else believed him. She felt very much alone clinging to her suspicions.

"I think I'm doing a pretty good job, Jodie," he told her earnestly. "I'm definitely committed to Allman Industries. I've told you before that I love this little town, and your father's company is making things better here for everyone. We all win."

Maybe he was right.

But then she remembered hints he'd given about his own family. "I know your mother isn't happy about you working for us. What about the rest of your family?"

"My father doesn't have an opinion. He hasn't been seen for six months. You did know he is taking an extended tour of Europe?"

"I'd heard that." She'd also heard that he and his father didn't get along, but that was hardly unusual.

"Tracy feels the same way my mother does. My uncle wanted me to come work the ranch with him, but…" He shook his head, his green eyes haunted. "No, I couldn't do it. That was not for me. Especially not working with my cousin Josh."

She made a face. It was strange to think of his family this way.

"I always thought of the McLaughlins as a sort of monolith," she said slowly. "I didn't know you all had disagreements among yourselves." She grinned suddenly. "I would have thought you'd have used up all that energy fighting with us all those years."

"You and all those brothers," he agreed with a nod.

"Yeah. And you with all those cousins." A picture of Jeremy flashed in her mind, but she pushed it away. "You outnumbered us two to one."

"Possible." His smile was teasing. "But we were the kind, magnanimous, open ones and you were the crafty, sneaking, back-biting—"

She brandished a small fist his way. "Watch it, McLaughlin. I can feud with the best of them."

His gaze seemed to glow, and he drawled out, "Oh, I'll just bet you can, Jodie Allman."

She found herself smiling into his eyes, and the moment held a few beats too long, until she was almost embarrassed, and looked back down at her work.

But it was hard to get her mind back on it again. Her thoughts were full of McLaughlins and Allmans—of Jeremy, and their secret, forbidden romance…of her father, and how hard he'd worked to get the business up and running in order to prove something to the McLaughlins…of her mother, and how she'd died much too young. Officially her mother had succumbed to cancer. But Jodie had always suspected she'd been vulnerable to illness because she'd been so worn down by the feud. The fight between the two families had colored all their lives for over a hundred years. And now here was Kurt, ready to bury it.

Did that make him a hero? Or a fool?

They wrapped up work in the early afternoon. Kurt had packed up the samples they'd taken from the grapevines, for shipment to the university, and Jodie was taking the package to the post office before swinging back by the office. He walked her to the door on his crutches.

"I haven't noticed you taking any pain pills today," she mentioned, hesitating on the doorstep. "Does that mean the pain has eased?"

He looked surprised. "Yeah, I forgot all about it. I did take a couple this morning, but I haven't needed anything since."

"Good." She still felt horribly guilty for having put him in this situation. But that didn't mean she was going to let up on him in other areas. "Now listen. When I get here tomorrow, I expect to see you fully dressed. Okay?"

He pretended to think that over. "Tell you what. I'll dress the way you want me to if you'll dress the way I want *you* to."

She couldn't help but laugh. "Why do I even bother to ask?" she beseeched of the heavens. But she did it anyway. "And what, pray tell, do you want me to dress in?"

"I've got a great idea," he said, eyes sparkling. "Remember that red halter top you used to wear? Is that still around?"

She stared at him. He remembered her in the red hal-

ter top. She felt her face turn as red as that piece of cloth-
ing had been, and she stammered something inane. He
remembered. He *had* been looking at her. It wasn't her
imagination. Reality seemed to ebb and flow around
her, but the sound of a car in the driveway brought her
quickly back to earth.

Chapter Six

"Oh," Kurt said in surprise. "We must be running late. It's my mother bringing Katy back."

Uh-oh. Jodie swallowed hard. She had to get out of here.

"Okay," she said, moving quickly. "I'll see you tomorrow."

"Jodie?" he called, but she didn't stop. She had to get to her car before someone tried to make her meet Katy. Her heart in her throat, she realized she was going to have to pass right by Kurt's mother.

Oh, well. If it had to be done, she'd better do it fast.

"Mrs. McLaughlin." She nodded with mock formality to the tall, handsome woman who had blackballed her from Junior Helpers League and who'd made sure she never got invited to any of the teenage parties everyone else in town attended at the McLaughlin mansion. Jodie didn't think she would ever warm up to this woman, especially after that time she'd heard her call the Allmans "trash" in that holier-than-thou tone.

"How are you?" she added, though she didn't pause in her determined trek toward her own car.

"It's Jodie Allman, isn't it?" the older woman said coolly, lifting her dark glasses to get a better look. "I'm fine, my dear. Thank you for asking."

Just as Jodie came even with the car, the woman turned and pulled Katy from the back. Jodie got a flash of blond hair and saw a chubby little hand wave in the air. The image stayed with her as she slid behind the wheel of her car and started the engine, trying to catch her breath.

Kurt's baby. A McLaughlin baby. That put an ache in the center of her being. Somehow it was just too close to home.

Dinner around the Allman table was loud and cheerful that evening, which was just what she needed to get her mind off Kurt and his child. It was one of those nights when her sister seemed extra loving, and her brothers were so funny she could hardly eat for laughing.

And then her father came down to join them. The laughter died away and everyone began to concentrate on finishing up so they could leave the table.

Jesse Allman went around the group, making comments that caused a lot of eyes to roll. And finally he fixed on Jodie.

"Well, missy," he said. "When I said you had to work with the McLaughlin boy, I didn't think you were going to move in with him."

She stiffened. "I didn't move in with him. We're just working together. I only go over for a few hours every day."

He frowned darkly. "I don't like it. I think you should stay at the office."

She'd thought exactly the same thing when all this had begun. But things had changed. She no longer thought that way.

"Dad, I can handle things. I'm an adult, you know."

He stared at her and she stared right back, until he began to chuckle.

Rafe rose from his place, giving her a significant look and taking his plate to the sink. "Dad, did you want to talk over some of those numbers from the Houston proposal?"

"Yes, I'm fixin' to do that as soon as you all are done here. Matt, I want you in on this."

"Sorry, Dad." Matt rose with a quick smile and followed Rafe to the sink. "I've got to get over to the Simpsons'. Their baby has a temperature and I said I'd come over and take a look."

Jesse scowled and Jodie hid a grin. No matter how much he tried to pretend otherwise, he had a son who was a physician. No matter how much he tried to push him, Matt would never be as interested in the family business as he was in his patients' health.

Too bad, Dad, she said to herself.

And then the phone rang, and she took that opportunity to make her own escape, hurrying out to the hall where the old, dial telephone was located.

"Jodie?"

The voice in the receiver was Kurt's, and her heart jumped. He was the last person she'd expected to hear from.

"Listen, if you're not busy….I'm going stir-crazy here. What about we go for a ride or something?"

"A ride?" It took a moment to process the unexpected request. "Oh, in my car?"

"Unless you've got a horse you need to exercise," he said dryly. "Yes, in your car. I can't drive."

"But…what about your baby?"

"Tracy took Katy with her to a friend's house. They have little kids. So I'm on my own."

She could hear it in his voice, a caged-in quality, as though he really needed to get out of the house. She could sympathize.

"I'll be over in twenty minutes," she said. As she hung up the phone, she got that old feeling of dread and regret. She was walking into a trap again, wasn't she? With her eyes wide open, her mind full of doubts—and her heart full of anticipation.

They didn't drive for long. It took only moments to decide to stop at Millie's for coffee.

"Are you sure you want to do this?" she asked, as

they prepared to go in. "You know people are going to talk."

"Sticks and stones," he said, a bit obliquely. "Who cares?"

Well, she did, for starters. But she swallowed her misgivings and held the door for him as he made his way in on crutches. He looked even better in the evening lighting than he did in sunlight. The hunter green sweater he wore emphasized his muscular form, and his thick hair was tousled by an evening wind blowing in off the plains. He was "to die for" great-looking and familiarity was breeding the opposite of contempt. Just catching his gaze made her pulse speed up.

"Besides," he said, looking around the half-empty restaurant, "there are so many new people in town, there probably won't be anyone here who remembers that McLaughlins and Allmans don't mix."

"You might be right," she said, but she was dubious.

There was definitely a different look to the place. The old Formica tabletops and red Naugahyde seat covers had given way to chrome and blond wood. Plants hung from the rafters where old hunting trophies had once glared down on the patrons. But Millie was still there to meet them, her face lighting up when she saw her daughter's best friend.

"Jodie!" she cried, rushing forward to give the younger woman a bear hug. "It's about time you came by to say hi."

After Jodie's own mother died when she was sixteen,

Millie had served as a substitute, of sorts, when times got tough to bear. They chatted warmly for a few moments, and then it was time for the big decision.

"Which side?" Millie asked, looking from one of them to the other.

Kurt and Jodie looked at each other. The side by the windows had always been McLaughlin territory. A smaller area toward the back had been staked out by the partisans of the Allman boys. The town was divided right down the middle, and so was the restaurant. Millie had her hands full in the old days, making sure that each faction kept to their own side and that the hostilities didn't spill over into real fighting in her establishment.

Jodie laughed and looked at Millie. "People don't still divide down the center line, do they?" she asked, incredulous.

Millie shrugged, a twinkle in her eye. "Some do. What about you two?"

"We'll take the booth in the middle," Kurt said smoothly. "Our relationship is a compromise, isn't it?"

"Absolutely."

Millie seated them and went to get their coffee. Jodie looked around the place, remembering coming here after football games, when the room was packed with friends and enemies. Two teenage girls passed the table, their gazes falling on Kurt. Their immediate reactions were almost comical, and their giggles echoed through the air as they made their way to the restroom in back.

Jodie hid a smile behind a napkin. "I didn't know you had groupies," she said, raising her eyebrows.

He grinned back at her. "It's a new thing. I don't like to advertise it."

She shook her head. "I'd be careful if I were you. It's pretty dangerous to depend on the fickle affections of the crowd."

"So what's new? Depending on the fickle affections of grown women isn't much better."

Jodie did a double take, wondering at the cynicism in his tone. But he'd already moved on to another topic, and Millie was serving the coffee.

A couple of people stopped by to say hello. The teenage girls passed again, giggling all the way. And Jodie began to feel as though she'd really come home. Funny that it took coming to Millie's with a McLaughlin to make that happen.

"I wish you'd stayed for another moment this afternoon," he said, as he sipped his black coffee. "I wanted to introduce you to Katy."

"Well, I thought it best if I…got going…."

"Yeah, I know. You and my mother have never been on the best of terms."

Jodie wrapped her fingers around her cup, soaking in the heat. "That's putting it mildly. Your mother hates me."

"Hates you?" He reacted automatically to the word, as though he were going to deny it vehemently. But then he reconsidered. "Well, only because you're an Allman."

"Exactly."

Their gazes met, locked and they both laughed. He reached out to take her hand in his, but she pulled it away quickly.

"No you don't," she said, looking around the room from under her lashes. "Just us having coffee together is enough to rile the town. If we start holding hands…"

He looked almost abashed. "I wasn't going to hold your hand."

"Really?" She didn't believe him for a moment. She picked up that very same hand and looked at it. "What were you planning to do with it, then?"

He shrugged, amusement lurking in his eyes. "Nibble on your fingers a little, maybe."

She gave him a withering look. "Better order a piece of pie if you're hungry."

But she was warmed by his flirting. And she thought again about how he'd noticed her in the red halter top all those years ago…and actually remembered it! She'd never forget that summer—coming into Millie's with her friends and sneaking glances at the college-bound boys, singling out Kurt every time and getting breathless just by catching sight of him. Had he been looking at her, too? She got breathless again, just thinking of it.

He had gone off to college at the end of that summer, and she hadn't seen him again until the day she walked into his office at Allman Industries and announced she'd come to work for him. By then, there had been a lot of water under the bridge.

Kurt was talking about his mother again, and the problems he was having with the child care for his baby. Things weren't going smoothly, and he was trying to figure out a way to improve the situation.

"Here's my big dilemma," he was saying, leaning across the table toward her and speaking quietly. "The puzzle that is tying my life in knots." He hesitated, then went on as though he'd decided he could trust her with his problems, after all. "How do I get a mother for Katy without having to hire on a wife for myself?"

"Hire?" She raised one eyebrow and stared at him, inexplicably offended by the way he was thinking of this.

He spread his hands out and looked at her candidly. "I don't see it happening any other way."

She studied him for a moment, then decided he wasn't serious. He was just being dramatic because he was so frustrated. "You'll meet someone," she told him confidently. "You'll fall in love."

"Oh, yeah." He gave her a look of pure disgust. "I already caught that movie. And the sequels are never as good as the original."

That stopped her short. She snuck a look at his face, expecting to see a hint of the anguish he must feel from having lost his wife. But his expression was bland. If he was in agony, it didn't show. In fact, she thought there was more of a bitter look to the twist of his mouth than anything else. Strange.

Everyone knew he and Grace had been the perfect couple. Everyone said he'd been heartbroken when she'd gone down in the small plane over the panhandle. Everyone wondered if he would ever love again.

Now Jodie was beginning to wonder if everyone knew what the heck they were talking about.

"You met Grace in college, didn't you?" she asked, knowing she was treading on shaky ground, and ready to retreat at the barest hint that he didn't want to discuss it.

He nodded. "We met in a class on fungi. There was a field trip every other Saturday, so we had a chance to get to know each other." His eyes took on a dreamy look. "She was beautiful. Long, silvery hair down her back, pale blue eyes. She looked like an ice queen." He shook his head, talking more to himself than to her. "I couldn't get enough of her."

Jodie looked away, just this side of embarrassed at the candor of his statement.

"So we got married as soon as I got my degree," he said more briskly. "And we moved to New York City and lived like jet-setters for a while. Then Grace got pregnant and everything changed."

His eyes were stormy now, clouded with some emotion Jodie couldn't quite identify—and wasn't sure she wanted to understand. She waited for him to go on, but suddenly, he looked up as though he'd only just remembered she was there. His eyes cleared and he smiled at her.

"Hey, enough of that. Tell me about your work as a physical therapist. What made you want to go into that, anyway?"

She started off slowly but soon gathered speed, telling him all about how she'd worked two jobs and got her classes in at night, until she qualified for a scholarship and only had to work one job to make enough to live on. They talked for another half hour, and then it was time to take Kurt home so he would be there when Tracy brought Katy back.

"She'll be asleep," he mused, almost to himself, as they drove down the wide street toward his neighborhood. "Tracy will carry her in, and her sweet little face will look so angelic."

Jodie looked at him sideways. It was very appealing, the way he loved his little girl, but it put a sick feeling in the pit of her stomach. There was no way she would ever have a relationship with a man who had children. It just wasn't in the cards for her. And she'd better not forget that fact.

She pulled up in front of his house and he turned to her, smiling in the dark.

"Thanks for rescuing me, Jodie. I really didn't think I would be able to stand another night clumping around in my living room. You gave me a welcome break."

"Anytime," she said breezily, though her attention was all on his luscious mouth, and whether or not he would try to kiss her again.

Stupid, she scolded herself silently. *This isn't a date. There is no reason for him to try to kiss you again.* That one kiss had been just a moment of insanity, never to be repeated again.

But she couldn't convince herself of that. Probably

because she wanted him to kiss her again. She wanted it more than she'd wanted anything for a good, long time.

The night sky was black by now. There was no moon yet, and tiny diamonds twinkled like holes in heaven. It was a Texas sky, big and bold and full of magic. Maybe if she wished on one of those stars…

His face was so close. His hand was in her hair again, his fingers kneading softly. His gaze was soft as velvet. "You know, Jodie…I really, really want to kiss you."

Her heart lurched. "Oh."

His mouth twisted. "I'm not going to kiss you, though."

She gazed at him in horror as he went on with his stupid explanation.

"Doing something like that would go against all my plans, all my principles. I've really tried to take a firm stand against—"

She'd had enough of this gibberish. Principles be damned! She wasn't going to let him go on this way, or even finish his sentence. Instead, she took a firm grip on his head, one hand on either side of his surprised face, pulled him down within range and kissed him.

"There," she said breathlessly when it was over. "Now was that so hard?"

He stared at her for one long second, and then he began to laugh. Reaching out, he gathered her up, pulled her to him, and his mouth came down hard on hers.

Bells were ringing. Stars were shooting in the sky like fireworks. Violins were playing. And her body was responding to the heat of his mouth by going into total meltdown.

When he finally pulled back, she heard a small, plaintive sound, and realized it was hers. She had actually whimpered. But she was too overwhelmed to feel embarrassment. Kurt was a man who surely knew how to kiss. And she wanted him to do it again! And again...

"Good night," he said softly, and then he turned to let himself out of the car.

"'Night," she echoed.

And then he was gone.

Gone, but never forgotten.

Of course, Jodie knew things couldn't go on like this. But she wasn't taking it all that seriously. All she was doing was rekindling a teenage crush she'd once had and almost forgotten about. She would get over it soon, surely.

Still, she was a little worried the next morning as she made her way to Kurt's house. What was going to happen during these many hours they were forced to spend together? Was it going to be possible to ignore the attraction that was simmering between them now?

It had to be done. They couldn't let it get in the way of business. Which was exactly why he'd resisted kissing her the night before. She understood that. And in some ways, she knew she should regret having forced the issue.

But she couldn't. Even if they never kissed again, she

would never forget how wonderful it had felt being in his arms.

Once at Kurt's house, she found she needn't have bothered with all the worrying. It seemed that Kurt's home was about to become a hub of activity, a sort of annex to the Allman Industries building downtown. The day was filled with people coming and going.

Rafe was already there when she arrived.

"Hi, sis," he said, barely looking up from his work. "I'm going over some figures with Kurt. Pull up a chair. If you want to help, start collating these forms."

Paula, the marketing secretary, dropped by to pick up some dictation tapes. A little later, Matt arrived to check out Kurt's leg, and then David showed up at the door with an extralarge pepperoni pizza.

"Well, I heard the whole family was gathering, so I knew you'd all be peckish by now," he said in his South Texas drawl. "Maybe we should give Rita a call and tell her to get over here?"

"Rita took Pop into San Antonio to see the oncologist," Jodie said quickly. "So she's not available."

"How is your father doing with the chemotherapy?" Kurt asked, glancing at Matt first, then Jodie.

She shook her head. "He's a fighter. He's pretty tired most of the time, but he has flashes of his old self, pretty much daily."

"That's good," he said, but he was looking into her eyes, and she knew he wasn't thinking about her father any longer.

"What, no red halter top?" he murmured to her when they both took a trip to the kitchen for a glass of water.

She laughed, leaning against the counter as she poured water from the pitcher. "I guess this boring old outfit is a disappointment, huh?"

Coming up behind her, he dropped a small kiss at the nape of her neck. "Nothing about you is disappointing," he murmured. Then he turned and left the room.

Okay, you can stop hyperventilating now, she told herself firmly.

But it took a few long minutes of calming down before she felt like herself again. When he came back into the kitchen to get something he'd forgotten, she snagged his arm to make him stay for a moment.

"Listen," she said, wishing he didn't look so kissable. "I know this is my fault. But we have to stop it."

She could tell that he knew exactly what she was talking about, but he waited for her to say it.

"We've got to keep things on a business level here," she said earnestly, searching his gaze for his thoughts on the issue. "You were right in the first place. I was wrong to…to force that kiss on you last night."

He grinned and reached out to give her a soft tap on the chin with his fist. "You're such a Jezebel," he said lightly. "I'm putty in your hands."

She started to protest, but he stopped her. "Don't worry, Jodie. I understand. And reluctantly agree. No more making out in the shadows." He touched her cheek, then dropped his hand and shook his head. "But you can't stop me from dreaming."

She took a deep breath as he left the kitchen, closing her eyes and leaning against the counter as though she needed it to hold her up. She had to get out of this, and she knew it. But her rebellious streak was showing up again. She was going to enjoy it while it lasted. Why not?

Meanwhile, her brothers were giving her significant looks, and an occasional snicker could be heard among them. That put her back up enough to make her snap at Rafe at one point, when Kurt was out of the room. "Did you really come over because you had work to do, or did you come to act as a chaperone?"

"Why not both?" he countered with a grin. Then the amusement faded from his face. "Actually, kiddo, the business has got some cash-flow problems right now. I needed to work some things out with Kurt. With Pop out of the picture for the time being, we've hit a few snags."

"Are you serious? I had no idea."

"Not to worry. I'm working on it." He smiled teasingly at her again. "Just enjoy your little oasis while you've got it. Before you know it, you and Kurt will be back in the office and the good times will no longer roll."

She made a face at him, but his words stayed with her. She'd assumed, once the business took off and became a success, that things would just keep getting better and better. Of course, that was silly and naive. Nothing good remained so without a lot of work behind it.

Kurt came back into the room, and Rafe looked up from the computer screen.

"By the way, I saw Manny yesterday. He was all upset about some trespassers. He wanted me to ask you about them."

"Me?" Kurt looked surprised.

"Yeah, he seemed to think you might know something about them. Says he ran them off, but they came back the next night. They're skulking around in the vineyards and he doesn't know why." Rafe shrugged, turning away. "You know Manny. He tends to get riled up pretty easily. He said at first he thought it was like *The X-Files,* and they were government men come to search for extraterrestrials."

"I hope he doesn't try shooting one of them," Jodie said. "He could end up making things really hard for himself."

"And even harder for the guy who gets shot."

"True."

She met Kurt's gaze and knew they were both thinking about that day in the vineyards. He smiled at her and she smiled back. Something flashed between them— some sort of special bond. She looked away quickly, but her heart was beating very fast. This was what it felt like to be a part of a couple. She only wished she had the courage to make it real.

"It seems like you're spending a lot of time out of the office these days," Shelley said, as she noticed Jodie piling up work to take with her.

It had been over a week since she and Kurt had taken the trip out to the vineyards, and they had developed something of a routine. Jodie went into the office in the morning and gathered up work, took it to Kurt's house, and they sat down at his dining room table and did what needed doing. Kurt made some phone calls. She typed up some letters. They broke for lunch, finished up loose ends, and she left to spend the rest of the day at Allman Industries.

That would have been an invitation to intimacy, one would think. But it hadn't worked out that way. Luckily. And not because they were staying true to their decision to cool it, but because other people kept showing up and interrupting what could have been a cozy time together.

And then the weekend had come. She'd never known two days to stretch out so long and lonely. She'd spent the entire time doing nothing but think about him. She liked the guy. She couldn't help it. She *really* liked the guy. And that was so dangerous. So why was she sticking around? Self-hatred? Masochism? Or just plain old weakness?

After all, it was more than just resisting the urge to touch him. Even if he might go for a little cuddling, he'd made it very plain that he wasn't interested in pursuing any sort of long-term relationship. But then, if anyone had asked her a week ago, she would have said she wasn't, either. And now that was all she could think about.

"You going over to Kurt McLaughlin's again?" Shelley added.

"Of course," Jodie told her with something of a wistful smile. "The man can't get along without me."

Shelley laughed, but quickly sobered and then began to look concerned. "You're not falling for the guy, are you?" she asked.

Jodie struck a pose. "Shelley, do I look like a woman in love?"

Shelley pretended to gaze deep into her eyes. "I don't know. I see a few hints of insanity deep down there."

"Don't worry. I'm having those removed as soon as possible. Minor surgery."

"Good." Shelley grinned, then looked serious again. "Just be careful, okay? The McLaughlins are notorious as love-'em-and-leave-'em sort of guys. It seems to be something in the gene pool with that family." Looking as though she regretted the note of bitterness that had crept into her tone, she smiled quickly and patted Jodie's arm. "I don't want to see you get hurt, sweetie. You deserve better than that."

"I won't get hurt, Shelley. Don't worry about me. I've known too many members of that family for too long to be fooled by anything they do."

She knew she sounded a bit defensive. But darn it all, she *was* feeling a little defensive, when you came right down to it. Watching Shelley walk away, she had to wonder if her best friend had really noticed something. Was it that obvious?

She slumped down into her ergonomically correct desk chair and sighed heavily. Kurt could be so darn appealing sometimes. And the truth was, she had a little crush. That was all. It was a very small crush, and no one ever had to know anything about it. And it probably all hinged on the fact that it had been so darn long since she'd had a man in her life.

But it would be a very good thing if she could get a transfer to another department and not have to be alone with Kurt every day. She was beginning to think that was the only thing that was going to save her from making a first-class fool of herself.

Not that anything had happened.

Not that anything was *going* to happen.

She went to his house every day, and he teased her and mocked her and made her furious. And then all of a sudden, her gaze met his and held for just a beat too long—and something stirred inside her, and she was breathing too hard and thinking about hot kisses and shooting stars. It wasn't fair!

At least she'd managed to avoid having to deal with his little girl. The baby had gone to her grandmother's every day by the time Jodie got there, and Jodie left before someone brought her back. Tracy came over in the evening to help him with the child. Jodie was on guard all the time against being asked to help with the baby herself. That was something she wasn't prepared to do. The very thought made her cringe.

But she didn't want Kurt to know that. It was just plain stupid to be so paranoid about Kurt's baby. But she couldn't help it. She would just as soon never have to meet the child.

She glanced at her watch, deciding to stop at the Coffee Cabin to pick up a couple of tall Breakfast Blends and some doughnuts to take over to Kurt's. She'd noticed he seemed to respond well to arrivals bearing gifts of food.

A sleek, and very expensive, blue sedan sat in Kurt's driveway when Jodie drove up. She didn't recognize it, but she had a pretty good idea whose it had to be. Kurt's sister would drive a car like that.

She looked down at the things she'd picked up at the coffeehouse. What now? Oh, well. They could share things if they had to. She hadn't seen Tracy for a long time. It would be nice to see an old friend again.

Ha. Who was she trying to kid? "Friends" was something she and Tracy had never been. Rivals, sure. Competitors. Even enemies. From the first day five-year-old Jodie had hesitantly stepped into the kindergarten classroom, Tracy was always trying to gather the other children into her camp and leave her Allman rival out of things. Every time there was a snake lurking in her desk, her homework papers disappeared or there was a birthday party she didn't get invited to, Jodie knew whom to thank.

But that was then and this was now. And the feud was supposed to be waning, wasn't it? Gathering the sweets and coffee, she got out of the car and started up the walk. She could hear voices coming from the house, but it wasn't until she was up on the front porch that she could understand what was being said.

"Kurt, you can't really expect Mother to go out of her way to take care of your baby when you won't even do what she thinks is right about this Allman business."

Jodie stopped dead. The front door was standing open, and the voice inside, raised high with emotion, had to be Kurt's sister.

"Tracy, you don't understand." The deeper, masculine voice was Kurt's.

"I think I understand only too well."

"When this is all over, you'll see why—"

"When this is all over, I hope I'll be living happily in Dallas, my only contact with Chivaree by e-mail for the rest of my life."

"This will always be your home and you can't change that. And you'll always care. Believe me, I know."

"No. I cared when this town was our oyster. Now that the Allmans have turned everything upside down, I hope the place goes to hell. I'm sure the Allmans will do their best to take it there."

"Tracy, calm down. You'll wake up Katy."

Jodie stood where she was, not sure if she should go on in or head back to her car. The conversation was private, and it was heated. But her family's name had been mentioned. She shifted her weight from one foot to another, undecided.

Tracy spoke again, her voice lower, obviously trying to get control of herself.

"Look, I know you keep trying to convince Mother that you're doing something here that is going to return our family to its former so-called glory. But I don't know why you care about that. This whole town is a dump. It always was and it always will be. If you think you're going to make things better by hanging around with those low-down, thieving Allmans, you just go right ahead and do it. I'm getting out of here. And I'm not coming back."

It was at that moment that Kurt noticed her, as he looked up over his sister's shoulder.

"Jodie."

She was numb. What Tracy had said was skittering around in her head, but she wasn't letting it penetrate. Instead, she started forward as though she'd just arrived on the scene.

"Good morning," Jodie said with forced cheer. "I brought coffee and doughnuts." She waved the bag, walked right in and put everything on the table. Then she turned with a wide smile to greet Tracy.

"Tracy. So good to see you again."

"Well, if it isn't Jodie Allman. You hardly look any different than you did in high school."

Jodie couldn't say the same about Tracy. She'd been such a pretty girl, and now she looked strained and a little hard, wearing too much makeup and too many pieces of flashy jewelry.

Still, she knew very well that Tracy's comment wasn't meant as a compliment, but that only made her smile more broadly.

"And you look just gorgeous. But then, you always were the prettiest girl in town, weren't you?"

"I don't know, Jodie." Tracy's smile gleamed unnaturally. "You were the one who beat me out for homecoming queen, weren't you?"

"A fluke." Jodie waved it away. "I think someone must have stuffed the ballot box."

"Oh, no." Tracy shook her head. "You deserved every one of all those honors you were racking up in those days."

"As I remember it, you did your fair share of blowing away the competition for everything from president of the junior class to queen of the grape festival." Jodie smiled, feeling like a mechanical doll. Looking back, it seemed that she and Tracy had fought it out for every one of those things. Sometimes Tracy won, sometimes Jodie did. Another battlefield in the old family feud. From this vantage point, it all looked a bit pointless.

But she noticed that Kurt was watching their exchange with a look of pure disbelief on his face, and she knew exactly what he was thinking.

Women! How can they act like best buddies when they hate each other? If this were a couple of guys, someone would have a shiner by now.

That made her laugh inside as Tracy prepared to leave. He just didn't get it. Everything she and Tracy were saying to each other was meant to hurt. Just tiny little paper cuts, but they stung. The two of them understood each other perfectly.

Just before Tracy went out the door, she turned back and landed her final bomb.

"Oh, I almost forgot to tell you, Kurt. Mother's hired a housekeeper for you. She'll do your cooking and cleaning and take care of Katy. I just can't do it anymore, and I won't allow you to get Mother more involved." Her teeth flashed in a smug smile. "In fact, I've convinced Mother to come to Dallas with me for the time being. So you'll be on your own."

Chapter Seven

Kurt looked pained as he leaned against the open door.

"A housekeeper?"

"She's very good. Wonderful references." Tracy waved a hand in the air and added, "She's Swedish," as though that explained everything.

"Swedish?" he said, eyes lighting up. "As in, the Swedish Girls Bikini Team?"

Tracy rolled her eyes and looked at Jodie as if to say, *"Men!"* Even though mortal enemies, they were both women, and therefore subject to mutual exasperation about the opposite gender.

"She's a housekeeper," Tracy said, carefully enunciating the word to make sure he understood. "I doubt very much she'll be wearing her bikini to work."

Kurt looked pathetically hopeful. "You never know. Those Swedish girls…"

After flashing him another look of complete irritation, Tracy glanced at her watch. "I do have to fly. She should be here by noon." Giving Jodie an arctic smile, she added, "Nice to have seen you again. We probably won't be having a repeat. I'm moving to Dallas. For good." She waved at the two of them. "Ta ta." And she was off down the walkway in her expensive Italian pumps.

Kurt and Jodie stood watching her go, then Kurt slowly closed the door, his face dreamy. "Swedish," he said softly. One eyebrow rose. "Hmm. This could be interesting."

Jody was feeling just as exasperated as his sister had been. "Or not," she muttered, heading for the table and the coffee.

"Well, you heard what Tracy said." He joined her, lowering himself carefully to the chair, his cast out straight before him. "They've hired a Swedish woman to come and 'do' for me."

She looked up and found his eyes were sparkling. He was teasing, goading her, hoping for a reaction. She supposed she might as well play along for the time being. He was getting such a kick out of this.

"What exactly are you thinking this Swedish woman is going to 'do' for you?"

He shrugged expansively. "Who knows? You know what they say about those Swedes. She may just be the kind of wonderful woman who wants to take care of the 'whole man.'" He sighed happily at the thought. "She may just be anxious to attend to my every little want, need and desire."

Jodie was tempted to roll her eyes, but Tracy had already done that, and she didn't want to be repetitive. Still, she had to do something. She decided to tease him back a little.

"I thought that was what I was here for."

That surprised him. "You!"

"Why not me?"

For a moment, she could have sworn he was tempted to take that further. But only for a moment. He seemed to remember that theirs was supposed to remain a working relationship, sometimes skating on the edge of flirtation, but never risking actual contact. As she watched, he opted for safety, taking a long sip of coffee and reaching for a doughnut.

"Know any words in Swedish?" he asked her as he munched, reverting back to the subject at hand.

Jodie blinked. "I'm sure she speaks English."

"Yes, but if I could welcome her with some words in her mother tongue, who knows? It might make her feel more at home."

Her impulse was to snarl at him. She wasn't sure why, but this was beginning to annoy her. "If she wanted to talk to Swedish people, she would have stayed in Sweden."

He nodded thoughtfully. "Good point."

Despite herself, Jodie started to laugh. This was all so ridiculous. She reached for another doughnut, but

Kurt reached out at the same time and snagged her hand, holding it in his.

"You look good when you laugh," he told her.

The laughter died quickly. His eyes were too serious. She looked down at his hand holding hers. His fingers were long and beautiful. She thought about what they would feel like on her body, and shivered.

"I know you heard what Tracy said about your family," he went on. "I'm sorry. She didn't really mean it. She was just…"

Exasperated, she pulled her hand away from his. "Oh, Kurt! How can you say she didn't really mean it? Of course she meant it. It's you who are not dealing with reality. The Allman-McLaughlin feud is alive and well and we're all a part of it. Face it."

He was shaking his head, rejecting her pessimism. "The only reason feuds like this keep going is because people keep saying things like this to each other. When people are always trying to score points against each other, nothing gets accomplished."

She shook her head slowly. "I don't know if you can say that. After all, the bad feelings come out of some pretty bad actions, not just from talk."

"Yeah? Like what?"

She stared at him. Surely he didn't think the feud was all based in head games and hurt feelings? There was a lot more to it than that.

"Don't tell me you've never heard about how your great-grandfather, Theodore McLaughlin, kidnapped my great-grandfather's wife and locked her up for weeks, only letting her go when Hiram—my ancestor—gathered enough men and weapons to storm the ranch house where he was holding her?"

Obviously, that story was coming back to him now. He looked just a mite pained.

"Okay, so there were some romantic shenanigans back in the Chivaree Stone Age. But our two families were practically the only people living in this valley at the time. Who else were they going to mess around with?"

She went on, her face set. "Then there was your grandfather stealing the lease to my grandfather's land."

He groaned. "Ancient history. And disputed history, at that. Can't we just move on?"

"Move on?" She threw her hands in the air. "Sure, why not. Let's move on to the day that your father and your uncle ganged up on my father and tied him to a post in front of the city hall in his underwear for everyone in town to see and laugh at."

He made a show of looking very bored. "They were teenagers. Are you done yet?"

Something about his manner told her she'd made her point. "Well, there are many more things I could bring up. But I'm done for now."

"Good." He favored her with a dazzling smile. "How about sharing that last doughnut?"

She sighed. He really couldn't handle the details of the feud. He really thought he could just wish it away, and all those old, dirty deeds could be assigned to a family history museum somewhere. Easy for him—his family was the perpetrator of most of the bad stuff. Her family, being the weaker in the old days, had been the victim. It was a little harder to forget when you were the one whose nose was rubbed in the dirt again and again.

Or was she the one being naive? Was there more to it than that? After all, her original suspicions had gone underground, but she hadn't proved them to be wrong in any way. Was all this just a cover-up for his real agenda?

She looked at him sharply, but the misgivings faded a bit once she took in his face. It wasn't just that he was good-looking. There was a sparkle in his eyes that made her want to smile, and a twist to his wide mouth that made her want to tease him. Either he was real good at hiding his true feelings, or she was going to have to admit he was coming across as a really good guy.

But then, she was nuts. What did she know?

"Hold still," he told her. "You've got sugar on your face."

She held still, scrunching just a little as he carefully wiped the sugar away. He was so close, she could feel the heat from his body. An overwhelming urge came over her to lean into his chest and bury her face against him. Her gaze met his, and she could tell he knew exactly what she'd been thinking.

His eyes darkened. He was going to kiss her. She drew her breath in sharply, knowing she should turn away. But she was frozen to the spot, heart beating, head light.

His arms came around her, drawing her into the shelter of his embrace. That was the way it felt, as though he was enclosing her in a magic space away from time and trouble. And beyond all reason, she let herself enter the dream. With a soft sigh, she lifted her own arms and circled his neck, pulling him closer, wanting to feel his body against hers. His mouth was hot and hard and she opened to him eagerly, thrilling to the sense of his obvious desire.

She knew this was crazy, but she didn't care anymore. It felt so right, so good, to be with this man. Was she falling in love? Was she really brave enough to let herself do that?

Drawing back at last, he looked down at her and she tried to read what his gaze was telling her. She could have sworn he looked a little shocked, a little disconcerted. Had her response surprised him? She didn't care. If he kissed her again, she would respond just as intensely.

But he didn't kiss her again. Instead, he asked, "So, you want to see Katy?"

"What?" Alarm shimmered through her veins. She'd forgotten that the baby was still here. "No. I…I mean, shouldn't we let her sleep?"

"Come on." He grabbed her by the wrist, hoisting himself up with one crutch. "I want to show you my pride and joy."

There was no way to avoid this, and it would be silly to try. Bowing to the inevitable, she forced a smile and went along with him into the bedroom at the end of the hall, her heart hammering in her chest. They entered quietly. The drapes were pulled but there was plenty of light. Jodie followed Kurt to the side of the crib and looked down.

Golden curls tumbled over a cheek round as an apple. The little mouth was slightly open. A small fist lay on the pillow. A tiny button nose. Fairy eyebrows. A beautiful, beautiful child.

Something like a sob choked Jodie. This darling, adorable little girl looked so much like the image she had of the baby she'd carried for four and a half months. Those days came flooding back to her. The long nights crying because Jeremy had abandoned her. The way those emotions had changed once she began to feel the presence of another life inside her. The way she'd taken her unborn baby to heart, loved it, vowed that she would do all she could to make sure the child had a happier childhood than she had had. They would be a pair, the two of them, mother and child.

And then, suddenly, that dream was dead, too. It had seemed too much to bear at the time.

She gripped the railing of the crib, trying to hold back the emotion. She was going to cry. Oh, no. This was totally unfair. She wasn't the crying type. At least, she tried hard not to be. And here she was, her eyes filling with tears, her shoulders shaking. She had to get out of here before he noticed.

Too late. He'd already seen it. She turned away but he pulled her back.

"Jodie, what is it?"

She could try to tell him a dismissive lie, but it wouldn't work. When your throat closed up, it was hard to get words through. Shaking her head, she pulled away from him and headed back out into the living room.

He followed her, clumping along with the crutch, but he was slower, and she had time to take a deep breath and wipe her eyes.

"You know," she said brightly, as he came into the room, "I really think I ought to go back to the office. I forgot to bring those new ad sheets you wanted to see. So if you think you can handle things here without me…"

"Sit down," he said, gesturing toward the couch.

"What?"

"Sit down. We need to talk."

"Oh. I don't think so. I'm okay, really, I just—"

"Sit down."

The tone was definitely autocratic and, as a modern woman, she knew she ought to challenge it. But somehow she found herself sitting down.

He sat beside her, grimacing as he stuck his leg out straight. Turning, he looked deep into her eyes.

"Jodie, tell me what happened to your baby."

Her heart lurched. "I…I've never had a baby."

His eyes darkened. "But you were pregnant."

She turned her face away. She couldn't deny that. And she felt like a fool.

"Tell me about it."

She shook her head. "Why? Why do you want to

know?" She shook her head again, harder. "Lots of women lose babies. It's no big deal."

He moved closer and took her by the shoulders, turning her so that she had to face him. "Remember when you told me that you liked me?" he asked.

She nodded, feeling like a child.

He touched her cheek and smiled gently. "Well, Jodie, I like you, too. I care about you. You're hurt, and I want to help you, just like you've helped me with my leg."

She searched his green eyes, looking deep, hunting for clues. Did he really mean it? Could she trust him? Or was it just that she wanted him to mean it?

She'd never told anyone the full story about what had happened ten years before. The man who was supposed to be her worst enemy should be the last person she told. Life was so strange sometimes.

"Kurt, I don't know…"

"Tell me."

She took a shaky breath. And with his hands still on her shoulders, warm and protective, she began.

"I took off right after high school. I had to get out of here." She looked down at her own hands, noting absently that her fingers were tangled together. Deliberately, she relaxed and let go.

"My mother died when I was sixteen, and that devastated me. I did nothing but fight with my father for the next two years. It was awful at home. I was sure anywhere else would be better. So I headed for Dallas as soon as I could scrape together the bus fare."

"It's a common story," he said, pulling her loosely into the circle of his arms. She let him. It felt right and natural, somehow.

"Yes," she said, as she settled against him. "And one that doesn't always have a happy ending."

"What happened?"

"Well. There was a boy."

"There's always a boy."

"Of course." She actually smiled for just a moment. "And I thought I loved him. Worse, I thought he loved me."

His arms tightened around her.

"We were sweethearts in high school. He came to join me in Dallas and we had a great time for a few weeks. But when I told him I…" She took another breath, suddenly having a hard time saying the word. "That I was pregnant, he let me know he had no intention of giving up the good life he'd just begun to sample." She winced, remembering. "He found it very amusing that I was so naive as to think he would marry me. He made it very clear that people like him didn't marry people like me."

Her voice wavered. Should she tell Kurt what he'd really said? Could she repeat it? No. But his words would echo in her ears anyway.

"Are you crazy, Jodie? It's a historical fact. McLaughlins sleep with Allman women, but they sure as hell don't marry them."

"I felt as though the earth had opened up and I was falling down through the core. There were times when

I couldn't catch my breath. I didn't know what I was going to do, where I was going to go. I lost my job and then I lived off soup kitchens for a while."

"Jodie…"

"And then I lost the baby." She shivered. "It was pretty messy. I was already in the fifth month, and it was bad." She looked up and met his gaze, and because he looked so sympathetic, she told him another thing she'd never told anyone else. "It's possible I won't ever be able to have children."

"Oh, my God." He pulled her in tightly, burying his face in her hair. "Oh, Jodie."

His comfort felt like heaven, but she knew it was a dangerous sort of paradise and she tried to pull back. "If you hold me like that, I'll start to cry again," she warned.

"Good," he said, smoothing back her hair. "You go ahead and cry."

She wasn't going to. She didn't want to. But his comfort destroyed her defenses, and she did.

But not for long. After all, this was all so stupid. How could she be so weak? Other women lost babies and they squared their shoulders and went on with their lives. They didn't develop phobias about being around children. What was the matter with her?

One thing was undeniable. She couldn't let a poor little defenseless baby bear the brunt of her own neuroses. It was way past time she faced this bit of squeamishness and conquered it. Somehow.

A crash came from the bedroom, and then a wail.

"Katy!" Kurt attempted to jump to his feet, forgetting about the cast, and fell onto the floor.

Jodie jumped up, too, and looked at where he lay, flailing like a turtle on its back. She turned toward the bedroom where the cry was coming from. She could stay here, pull Kurt to his feet and hope he hadn't hurt anything. Or she could skip the delay and go to the baby herself. Split seconds passed, but it felt like huge, long moments were hanging in the air.

And then she was moving. She never thought it out, exactly. She didn't plan it. She didn't even tell herself that it had to be done. But she did it.

She ran for the bedroom. Katy was on the floor, holding one hand to her head and crying as though she'd been abandoned. Huge tears were rolling down her round cheeks. But the minute she caught sight of Jodie, the crying stopped dead and she stared, fascinated.

"Are you okay, honey?" Jodie asked, bending down but not sure if she should touch her. "Did you get hurt?"

"Da da da," the baby said. She gave Jodie a penetrating look and made up her mind. Her little, chubby arms shot up over her head and she waved them at Jodie, begging to be held. "Da da da," she repeated, adding a little sob at the end.

Jodie licked her dry lips and looked back toward the doorway, hoping to see Kurt arriving. "You want to go to your da da… I mean, daddy? He will be here in a second if you just wait—"

"Da da da!" The arms waved more vigorously, and

the baby got the look of a very determined chipmunk about to launch itself into space if someone didn't do something to facilitate travel immediately.

"Okay, okay." Jodie bent down and reached for the child, not sure how this was going to be accomplished. But Katy helped and, in no time at all, she was firmly ensconced in Jodie's arms, and Jodie was breathing hard.

"Oh!"

She was holding a baby and she wasn't throwing up. She wasn't going to faint. She wasn't even going to make faces. Because it wasn't hard at all.

She turned as Kurt entered the room. She couldn't believe how wonderful this little princess felt in her arms. "Look," she told him, her face shining. "Here she is. I think she's okay."

Kurt stopped and looked at them, wearing a crooked smile. "I guess she's taught herself at least part of the way of how to climb out of the crib," he said, his green eyes taking in every nuance. "A new problem to deal with."

But Jodie didn't want to hear about problems anymore. She handed the baby over to Kurt, but she didn't move away. Instead, she stayed close, brushing the curls back off the baby's forehead, taking in the beauty of the child and resonating to it.

So many years of avoiding the issue, and once she confronted her greatest fear head-on, it filled her with a feeling of triumph. Cowardice didn't pay. That was a good lesson to learn.

They spent the next hour with Katy. Though she

would always have an ache in her heart when she thought of the baby she'd lost, she was learning to enjoy watching Kurt interact with the child. And she even enjoyed it a bit herself.

After all, who could resist Katy? She was a laughing, bubbling bundle of pure joy, exploring everything, reacting to all stimuli, so surprised with the tiny details of everyday life. Jodie just couldn't be sad with such a beautiful baby at the center of attention.

All this made Jodie wonder about something else. And as time went by, she worked up the nerve to ask Kurt about it.

They had been sitting around in a sort of circle, rolling a ball to the baby. The ball had stopped in the middle, making Katy laugh and clap her hands. Kurt leaned in and got it rolling again.

"When you look at Katy, does she remind you of Grace?" Jodie asked softly. "Do you miss her an awful lot?"

"No." He looked up from Katy, his eyes clear. "I don't miss Grace at all."

Jodie sat back. She'd had a few hints that maybe his marriage hadn't been as special as people said, but this total aloofness was a surprise.

Kurt shifted his weight so that he could turn toward her more easily.

"In fact, the truth is, if Grace hadn't died, I probably would have divorced her by now."

"Oh, Kurt." She had a guilty twinge. She had to

admit, if he'd teared up and pledged unending love for his late wife, she would have been tortured by such a declaration. So what was she supposed to feel now? Elation? Hardly that. And she hated to think of Kurt being unhappily married. But at the same time, she couldn't help but be glad he wasn't as grief-stricken as some would have said.

"The only thing that was holding me back," Kurt said, "was trying to figure out how I could do it without risking losing Katy."

Jodie shook her head. "Kurt, I'm sorry. I shouldn't have brought it up. It's really none of my business."

His eyes seemed to burn into her as he gazed at her for a long moment. "But it is, Jodie," he said softly.

Chapter Eight

Before he could elaborate, the doorbell rang.

Jodie looked at Kurt and they both said it at the same time.

"The Swedish housekeeper!"

Kurt used his crutch to leverage himself to his feet and went to the door. Just before he opened it, he gave Jodie a significant look and she had to smile, knowing what he was hoping would be on the other side. He opened the door with a flourish. And then took a step backwards.

The woman who stood on the doorstep was at least six feet tall, and looked as though she might choose trying out for an NFL team as her second career. The steely blue eyes that stared out from under a granite brow brooked no nonsense. She carried a small overnight bag and wore a heavy sweater, though the day had turned very warm.

"I am Olga," she said in a thick accent. "I come to take care of the baby."

"What?" Kurt stepped forward again, and it looked like he was considering barring the door. His dream of a nubile Swedish maiden had apparently just gone up in smoke. "I...are you sure?"

"Where the baby?" She took a step toward the doorway and Kurt took a step back again, then glanced at Jodie as if asking for help.

"Uh... Listen, I don't think we've decided yet just what sort of help we're going to need," he said, obviously grasping at straws. "Maybe you could leave your number and we'll call you...."

Olga wasn't one to wait around for an invitation. Pushing Kurt back brusquely, she came striding into the house.

"I know babies, Mister," she said, fixing him with a glare. She dropped her overnight case and looked around the room. "You let me have that baby. I take care of 'em."

Two long strides brought her to where Katy was playing on the floor. Leaning down, she picked the baby up and held her out while she fixed her with a fierce look. "She goin' to be okay."

Katy looked stunned. She glanced at her father, then back at this woman-mountain who had her in its grasp. Her little mouth opened, but she didn't make a sound.

"Which way to baby's room?" Olga demanded. "Needs new diaper."

Jodie pointed silently and the woman thundered off.

Kurt started after them, then turned back to look at Jodie. "Help," he said in a rather small voice.

Jodie laughed and grabbed his arm. "Let the woman do her job," she told him. "Tracy said she has excellent references. And I'm sure your mother wouldn't hire someone unqualified. Relax."

He stood restlessly before her. "You really think she's going to be okay?"

Jodie nodded. "Sure. Give her a chance."

He paced, muttering his doubts, and she hid her smile. Olga returned with Katy slung over her arm, looking shell-shocked and holding her arms out for her father's comfort.

"I'll go see the kitchen," Olga said cheerfully as she handed the child off to Kurt.

"Uh, Olga," Jodie said. "Mr. McLaughlin was wondering what exactly his mother had hired you on for. We assume it includes baby-tending and cooking."

"Oh, yah. Some cleaning, too. And I do massage."

"Massage!"

Olga laughed and gestured toward Kurt. "Come here. I give you a good one."

Jodie caught the look of pure horror on Kurt's face. It was a sight so precious, she would preserve it in her memory forever, bringing it out on cold winter nights to warm her soul.

"No, thanks," Kurt said grimly. "I think the baby care and housekeeping will be enough for now."

Jodie accompanied Olga to the kitchen and gave her a quick tour of the cabinets and appliances. Strangely, she felt an almost proprietary sense of things. She'd only been coming here a week or so, but she felt like it was hers.

Olga seemed fine to her. A bit bossy, perhaps, and a little loud—but competent and basically a good person. Definitely reliable. So she gathered her things and prepared to go back to the office.

"You're not leaving, are you?" Kurt said with alarm.

She had to smile. For a grown man who she'd seen square off against men twice his size, he was acting very skittish about this housekeeper.

"I've got to get going," she said blithely.

Kurt followed her to the door. "You can't leave me here alone with her," he whispered, looking back over his shoulder.

Jodie bit her lip, but then shook her head. "Oh, I can. And I will."

It wasn't pure sadism on her part. She had to go. She needed some time to process the changes she'd gone through today. Any more, and she would have gone into overload mode, and a catatonic state couldn't have been far behind.

"Jodie." He caught her arm and pulled her back, looking down into her eyes. "Come back soon."

Something in the intensity of his voice stayed with

her all the way to the office. Darn it all! She was falling for the guy, big time.

"Oh, happy day," she muttered to herself sarcastically.

"So I hear Tracy McLaughlin is planning on getting married again."

Dinnertime at the Allman house was Rumor Central these days. Jodie glanced up at her older sister and realized that statement had been directed at her. Of course.

"So it seems," she said casually, hoping to head off a larger discussion of the issue. "Pass the salt, please."

"What is this?" Matt commented. "Marriage number three?"

Rita nodded. "Hope she has better luck this time."

"Ha!" Rafe threw in. "McLaughlins never stick with anyone. Look at the parents. Not exactly the role models you would choose."

Rita waved a fork at her brother. "As I remember, you once had a pretty fair-sized likin' for Tracy."

"Me?" His handsome, dark face looked aghast. "No. I never had any feelings like that for a McLaughlin. I'm no traitor."

Jodie's jaw dropped. "Listen, y'all are sitting around bad mouthin' McLaughlins, but you think nothing of having Kurt work at the business. You want to explain that one to me?"

David shrugged as though it weren't even worth trying to explain. "Well, see, Kurt isn't like the others."

"Naw, he never has been," Rafe chimed in. "He and I were lab partners in chemistry in high school, and after the original snarling at each other, we got along fine. I always knew he was a good one."

"Not like those cousins of his. Every one of them is a skunk," David declared.

"I wouldn't turn my back to a single one of them," Matt added.

"No, Kurt's a good guy," Rita agreed. "I said as much when he came back home to Chivaree to raise his kid right. After the way his wife treated him…" She glanced at Jodie and her voice trailed off.

"Yes, go on." Jodie leaned toward her. "After what way his wife treated him?"

Rita sighed. "You didn't know?"

"If I knew, I wouldn't be asking, now would I?" Jodie looked around, realizing everyone seemed to know about this except for her. "From what I heard, she died in the crash of a small private plane. Is there more?"

The others looked at each other as though trying to decide who should be the one to tell her. Rita took over the story, by default.

"Well, from what they say, she was running off. Leaving him and the baby."

"Oh." Her heart lurched with pain for Kurt.

"She was on her way to meet her boyfriend when the plane crashed in the mountains."

"Oh." Jodie went cold. She'd had no idea. No one had said a word, least of all Kurt. Still, he had let her know things hadn't been good with his marriage. So this shouldn't be a big surprise. And it certainly explained that haunted look in his eyes on occasion. And his vow never to love again.

Well, he'd never actually said that. But she knew it was implicit in his attitude toward ever marrying again. It must have been agony for him to have the baby that he loved and wanted so badly, and have the baby's mother betray him just when he needed her most. She had a real surge of empathy for that one.

She couldn't eat any more after hearing this story. Her siblings went on to another subject, but she was silent. She wanted to go to Kurt, wanted to comfort him somehow. But anything along those lines was playing with fire, and she knew it. So what could she do?

They had all barely finished dinner when the phone rang and Kurt was on the line.

"Jodie. Thank God you're there. You have to come over right away."

"Why? What's happened?"

"I'll explain when you get here."

She frowned, her hand tightening on the receiver. He really did sound as though something terrible had happened. "Kurt, where is Olga?"

There was a pause, then Kurt said firmly, "Jodie, you've got to fire her for me."

Jodie's eyes widened. "Where is she?"

"I've…got her in a safe place."

"Kurt! Where?"

She could hear him taking a deep breath before answering. "I locked her in the laundry room."

"Kurt!"

"I had to do it. She was going crazy."

"What did she do?"

"I'll explain once you get here. Come quick."

She couldn't imagine what Olga could have done. Poor Katy! Jodie got angry in her own right. How could an adult do such a thing to a poor, defenseless little child. What exactly that "thing" was, she wasn't sure. But it had to be bad for Kurt to have locked the woman in the laundry room. She hurried over with her heart in her throat.

"Okay, tell me," she said as she burst into the house. "How is Katy? What did Olga do to her?"

"Look." He gestured toward the high chair, standing by the table and covered in a gooey-looking reddish-purple substance. "She was making her eat beets."

He said it as though he were talking about bamboo shoots under fingernails, and henchmen arriving with cat-o'-nine-tails slapping against their steel-protected palms.

"Making her eat beets?" Jodie repeated, thinking she couldn't have heard correctly. Or maybe, because she didn't know much about babies, she didn't realize the significance of this. She turned back to look searchingly at Kurt.

He nodded, outrage burning in his gaze. "Katy hates beets. She always has. She screams when she sees them coming. And that woman was forcing them on her."

Jodie blinked. "Forcing them?"

"She said babies have to be taught they can't get away with not liking certain foods. Poor Katy was crying as though her little heart would break and that…that woman kept stuffing beets into her mouth."

Jodie turned away. She really didn't know what to say. But one thing was certain—Olga wasn't working out. She and Kurt just didn't jibe.

"Okay," she said, her voice choked. "I'll go down and talk to her." She looked at him. "But Kurt, what are you going to do without someone to take care of Katy?"

"I've got that covered," he said simply. "You can stay and help me out."

The nerve of the man!

That phrase kept running through Jodie's mind. Funny, though, that instead of making her angry, it made her laugh. It was awful nervy to expect her to drop anything that might be going on in her life and come take care of his. But he did it with such open innocence, she couldn't take offense.

Besides, he wouldn't be in the predicament if she hadn't caused the accident. So she did owe him some consideration. Still, to casually assume that she would be there if he needed her…it took her breath away.

And that was the point. He needed her. Katy needed her. And—this was a new revelation to her—she loved being needed.

She handled the firing of Olga with skill and tact,

if she did say so herself. She explained to the woman that Kurt was under great stress and not functionally sound at the moment—that he had abandonment issues and certain irrational phobias that made it imperative that she, as a therapist, take over his treatment for the time being. The fact that her therapy training was in the physical, not the mental, realm was something Olga just didn't need to know. Bottom line, she convinced the woman that Kurt just wasn't ready to give up the care of his daughter to a real professional quite yet.

"Oh, yah," Olga said. "He is off his rocker. I could tell that." She made a derisive sound as she pointed a finger at her head. "And he going to spoil that baby rotten. You better watch 'em."

"Oh, I will," she told the woman as she escorted her out the front door, with Kurt nowhere to be seen. "I'll watch him like a hawk. Please send a bill for your services."

"Oh, no. Mrs. McLaughlin, she gave me a nice check already. Give me a call when the man get better, okay? He gonna need a woman like me to take over his life. You betcha."

"I…I'm sure he'll be thinking about you as soon as he's ready to take that step," she said, waving goodbye and sighing as she closed the door. "There you go," she said to Kurt, who came around the corner, holding Katy in his arms. "Got any more dragons you need me to slay?"

"My hero," he said with obvious relief. "Listen, I didn't mind shoving her into the laundry room, it was just talking to her that gave me the willies. She wouldn't listen to a word I said."

"Don't worry," Jodie teased. "She'll be back to take over your life once you are well enough to accept her services."

Kurt talked straight at Katy. "We're moving and leaving no forwarding address, aren't we girl?"

"Da da da," she agreed companionably.

He looked up, his eyes warm. "But we're taking Jodie with us. Okay?"

"Da da da." Katy gave a jump in his arms as emphasis for the last "da," and they all laughed.

"Will you stay?" he asked as they sobered. "I hate to ask you, but I don't have much choice."

She searched his eyes. They were troubled, and she knew he was as reluctant to risk being close to her as she was to him. She bit her lip. She knew what she ought to do. But she also knew what she wanted to do. Desire won out over mature thinking.

"Of course I'll stay," she said. "But just for tonight."

Chapter Nine

Three days later she was still there, and wondering if she would ever get up the gumption to leave. Not only was she madly in love with Kurt, she'd fallen under the spell of his little girl, as well, and she couldn't imagine giving up caring for her to anyone else.

Still, it had to happen. Once Kurt had his cast off and was wearing a knee brace instead, things would go back to normal for him. He and she would both go back to work at the office. And someone would have to be hired to care for Katy.

But she didn't want to think about that. They made a happy little family, the way things were. She slept in the third bedroom. In the mornings, she got up and went straight to Katy, who was usually gurgling happily and playing with her crib toys. After changing her, she carried her into Kurt's room, where he would sleepily accept his little sweetie while Jodie went into the kitchen to start something for breakfast and try to forget how sexy Kurt had looked with sleep in his eyes. By the time breakfast was ready, Kurt would have Katy in her high chair, and begin feeding her. They sat around the table for at least an hour, laughing and playing with the baby. She was such an irresistibly sunny child.

After breakfast, Kurt gave Katy a bath while Jodie cleaned the kitchen and set things up for the workday on the dining room table. Kurt put Katy down for a nap, and they would get in an hour or so of work before Katy woke again and called out for someone to come get her.

The rest of the day, they played it by ear. Work was interspersed with taking care of Katy's needs or playing with her. Other people dropped by, either with business or just to say hi. In the afternoon, they would go for a drive and stop at a park so that Katy could run through the grass and watch slightly older children on the play equipment. In the evening, the adults usually got takeout of one kind or another, while Katy had baby food from jars, and a bottle.

And once she was in bed for the night, Kurt and Jodie were on their own.

Sometimes the night would start with a movie in the DVD player, sometimes with a board game or a crossword puzzle. But no matter how things began, no matter how much Jodie vowed it wouldn't happen, every night she and Kurt ended up in the same position—in each other's arms.

She knew it had to stop. It was going nowhere, and she was asking for trouble. But it felt so good to feel his arms around her and have him whisper scintillating things in her ear. He was everything she'd ever wanted in a man. In fact, he'd turned her around in many ways. If he ever got to the point where he wanted a real relationship…

Oh, who was she kidding? There were just too many things between them for that ever to work. He didn't want to marry again. He'd been betrayed by the woman he'd chosen, and she knew him well enough by now to know that he felt as though he'd taken his shot and that was over.

He liked her. She could tell when a man liked her. And he liked the way she related to Katy. In fact, he told her every day that he'd lucked out having her as an assistant. But as for marriage—well, that was something else again.

She wondered, sometimes, if the feud was part of his reluctance, as well. He claimed he never gave it a thought, but how could you throw away something that had been embedded in you from the day you were born? She knew it still ate at her sometimes. She had moments, even now, when she wondered about Kurt, wondered about his motives in working for the Allmans. His explanation that it was the best job he could get seemed plausible, but just the same…

Tonight, with Katy tucked away in bed, they were snuggling on the couch. Kurt was lying down with his head in her lap, and she played with his thick, curly hair. He'd just been telling her about the Saturday before, when Manny's son Lenny had come over to play with Katy, and the two of them had fought over a toy.

"I guess the social skills don't come naturally at this age," he said, laughing at the scene as he remembered it. "I couldn't believe it when Katy picked up a plastic block and bopped poor Lenny on the head."

"And you thought she was too demure?" Jodie said. "I guess you haven't noticed the banshee shrieks she can give when she thinks she's not going to get her way."

"You're not trying to imply my little angel is spoiled, are you?"

"No. But she's no shrinking violet, either. Just a normal, healthy little girl." She smiled down at him. "You're going to have your hands full with that little darling as she gets older." They had just finished up a game of Scrabble, and she had won, so she was feeling a little cocky. "Girls rule, you know."

"Hey, you're starting to make me feel outnumbered already."

That would only work if she hung around too long. And that wasn't going to happen. Taking a deep breath, she changed the subject.

"Say, did you ever get back to Manny about those trespassers he was so worried about?" she asked, running her fingers through his hair and loving the way it sprung up to her touch.

"There's no problem," he said, reaching up to brush a strand of hair back behind her ear, his fingertips leaving shock waves behind. "I know who they were."

She managed to hold back the gasp his touch brought on, but she still ended up sounding a little squeaky as she said, "Really? Who?"

"They were from the university." Turning, he pulled up to a sitting position beside her. "The Botany department." His arm slid around her shoulders and his breath tickled her ear. His tongue flickered out and tasted her ear lobe. "They wanted to get more samples, that's all."

"Oh," she said breathlessly. "Okay."

She swallowed hard. This was where she should pull away and tell him the kissing had to stop. But her muscles felt like rubber bands, and her mind was turning to mush.

"Mmm," he purred, as he began to drop tiny kisses down the cord of her neck. "Okay is not the word for this. Magnificent might apply, though."

She was melting. She always melted at his touch. She turned her head to protest. "Kurt…"

His mouth stopped her words in her throat. Closing her eyes, she let his heat fill her, like a shot of brandy on a cold winter's night. The man set her off like nothing she'd ever known before. His kisses were intoxicating, drugging, addictive. She let the sensation flood through her, luxuriating in the magic, wanting to stretch her body out, wanting to feel him against her.

But this wasn't what she'd planned. Slowly, she forced herself to emerge from the spell of it. She had to stop this now or she would be lost in his silken net forever.

"Kurt, stop."

His hand cupped her cheek. "I don't want to stop."

"I don't either, but…Kurt, you have to stop. We can't go on like this."

"But we can, Jodie. And once I get this cast off, we can go even further."

The shock of that thought gave her a surge of strength. "No. Stop."

He pulled back and looked at her, his green eyes unreadable. "What's wrong?"

She rose from the couch, looking down at him in despair. "Kurt, this is crazy. We started out being perfectly honest with each other. Neither one of us was looking for a romance. I don't know quite how this happened…."

"I'll tell you how it happened." Reaching out, he grabbed her hand. "It's an ancient tale, replete with hormones and moonlight. We hung out together and found we're attracted to each other. End of story."

She closed her eyes and shook her head before glaring down at him again. "You see, that's just the problem. That 'end of story' thing you just said. This shouldn't be an end. This should be a beginning. And since it's not, the other stuff is just treading water."

He looked at her quizzically. "The other stuff being…?"

She sighed sadly. "The physical attraction thing."

"Ah. The urge to merge."

"Kurt!" She threw up her hands. "You see? It's no use. We can't even talk frankly about these things without you making a smart-aleck remark. We just don't have a future together, do we?"

She waited, every nerve on edge. If he'd changed his mind, if he really had developed a new opinion, now was the time for him to say so. Her heart beat in her throat and she waited. And waited. But when he finally responded, it wasn't with the words she'd hoped for, and her heart sank.

"I'm sorry," he said calmly. "Really. I didn't realize you were taking this quite so seriously."

She stared at him. So it was all fun and games to him?

"Oh!" Jodie said. Without another word, she turned on her heel and stomped off.

"You know, day after tomorrow Rafe is taking me into San Antonio for a series of X-rays," Kurt told her later as they were having a last-minute cup of tea in the kitchen. "It's likely the doctor will shift me over to the brace."

Then it was almost over. She turned to look at him, a fist-sized ache starting up in her stomach. What he'd said earlier about her taking their relationship too seriously was still echoing in her head. He was right, of course. She'd known from the beginning nothing long-term could come of this. "We'd better make some plans, then," she said, maintaining a cool outward appearance. "We're going to have to find day care of some sort for Katy."

It wasn't until he looked at her with one eyebrow raised that she realized she'd said "we." She flushed. Well, that pretty much gave the charade away, didn't it? She did think of them all as a "we." If only he did.

"Not Olga," he said. "Might as well send Katy off to military school."

"Poor, misunderstood Olga." Jodie shook her head. "Okay, if not Olga, who?"

He frowned. "Don't you know any older women who might do it?"

She shook her head again. "Not really."

"How about your sister?"

"Rita? No, she's got her hands full with Pop right now." She frowned, thinking hard, then remembered something. She turned to look at him. "I was thinking.... Kurt, tell me this. How do you get along with your cousins these days?"

"My cousins?" He looked as though, had she not reminded him he had some, he would have forgotten all about them. "Some of them, great. Some okay. And one doesn't bear talkin' about."

She looked at him sharply but she didn't pursue it. She'd been thinking that someone who was related to Katy would be better than a stranger. So, if any of the cousins were available, that might be an avenue to pursue. "What's happened to all those cousins, anyway? Are any of them still around here?"

"Sure. Josh is managing the ranch, and trying to bring it out of the hole my uncle and my father ran it into. Jason's in San Antonio, running McLaughlin Management. Kenny and Jake are in the Middle East. They're both Special Ops. Jimmy and Bobby are both in college. And Jeremy…"

His voice trailed off. She waited, heart thumping. *What about Jeremy?*

"I guess Jeremy doesn't come home much these days, does he?" she ventured hopefully. *Oh, please, tell me he's on a ten-year safari to the heart of the African jungle,* she thought. *Please tell me not to expect him back here ever again.*

"No, I don't think even Jeremy would have the nerve to come back here," Kurt said, a sudden touch of bitterness lacing his words.

She looked at him quickly. Did he know? But he wasn't looking at her. He was staring off into space, as though he had his own bad memories of Jeremy. Well, that she could believe. Jeremy was bad news all the way around.

Suddenly he turned back, leaned across the table and took her hand, staring deep into her eyes.

"The man who left you high and dry when you were pregnant was my cousin Jeremy, wasn't it?"

He said the words softly, but there was a deadly menace behind them that made her shiver.

"How did you know?" she asked him, feeling very much alone. It was something she hadn't told anyone about, and she wished it were something she could forget.

"Jeremy told me. Well, he didn't actually name you, and didn't give me all the details, but he told me enough for me to guess it had to be you."

The jerk. He couldn't even keep his mouth shut. She nodded. "It was me."

"I'm sorry, Jodie. Jeremy is a regular bastard. I wish there was some way I could make it up to you." He hesitated, then went on, his eyes hooded. "There's just one thing I've got to know. Do you still love him?"

Her head whipped around. "Who? Jeremy? Oh, my gosh, no."

He was gazing at her intently. "Are you sure?"

"I haven't seen him in ten years. And I haven't wanted to see him."

"He hasn't ever contacted you?"

She looked at him and raised her chin. "Not since the night he told me that McLaughlins don't marry Allmans."

Kurt went still as a statue. "He said that?"

She nodded. "Don't worry about it. The sting has pretty much worn off after all this time. And I don't hold it against you, for heaven's sake."

Groaning, he reached out and pulled her into his arms, then into his lap.

"Jodie, Jodie. I wish I could wash away all the bad things that ever happened to you."

She sighed, wishing that, too. But just being held by him went a long way toward fixing everything.

He kissed her, and that made things even better. She

opened to him, savoring the sensation of his lips on hers as she teased his tongue. Then the heat began to build, and she was gasping as the kiss turned passionate. His mouth was everywhere, branding her with his lips, and she shivered with a new delight that she'd never known before. When his hand slid under her shirt and tugged on her bra, she stretched back to give him access, whimpering as he found her nipple and teased it between his fingers. There was a fire within her, a fire that was going to smolder until she had him inside her to quench it. The deep throbbing had begun, and she knew she had to stop things or…

"Okay," he said huskily, his mouth against her neck. "That's enough. For now."

They pulled apart and she looked at him, bleary-eyed and out of breath.

"Oh, boy," she said, for lack of anything more intelligent being able to penetrate her love-wracked brain. "Oh, wow."

He laughed, pulling her close again. "Jodie Allman, you crack me up," he said.

But his eyes said that she did more than that. And she was tingling with the joy of it for hours afterwards.

They took Katy to the park the next day, and someone mistook them for a real family. They pretended no mistake had been made, and it deepened the bond that was developing between them. Jodie put Katy into the protective seat, and Kurt stopped her before she got in the car to drive them home. He dropped a kiss on her lips.

"You know how I once told you that the only way I would ever get a mother for Katy would be to hire one?"

"I do, indeed."

He was smiling, but there was a strange light in his eyes that made her wonder.

"Well, here's the deal. How much would you charge?"

She stared at him, appalled. She knew he had to be joking, but she didn't find it very funny. Was he actually talking about hiring her to be a mother to his child?

"I'm serious," he was saying, the merriment fading from his eyes and a new look taking over, as though what had started as a joke now looked like something to consider. "I know I'll never have another chance to hire anyone who fits the bill like you do."

She gaped at him. "Do you know how insulting that is?"

He looked surprised. "Why? Because I made you a straightforward offer? I suppose you'd rather I asked you to marry me?"

If ever a fellow needed a thumping! "You can ask anything you like, Kurt McLaughlin. I'm not marrying anybody. Not for love, nor money. So keep your silly ideas to yourself." She flung herself into the car.

"I'm not marrying anybody, either," he said grumpily as he got into the passenger seat.

"Then I guess we're even."

"I guess we are."

They glared at each other all the way home.

* * *

The next morning Jodie saw Kurt off to San Antonio, with Rafe driving. She waved as they disappeared, then went back into the house and began picking up things in the living room. The testy mood that had begun the day before was still with her. Today would probably be her last day in this house. Once she and Kurt went back to the office, would their relationship shift back to what it had been originally? Maybe it should.

She'd hardly begun tidying up when the phone rang. It was Manny Cruz.

"Hi, Jodie. You got Rafe's new number? I want to call him about something."

Rafe had just moved into his own apartment. His brothers were teasing him about wanting some privacy to improve his social standing with the dating set. And truth to tell, he didn't deny it.

She gave Rafe's old friend his new number but added, "You won't catch him today. He took Kurt in to San Antonio to see the doctor."

"Oh." Manny sighed deeply. "Maybe I ought to go ahead and tell you," he said.

Her ears perked up. "Sure. Tell me. I'll help you if I can."

"Okay," he said, sounding reluctant at first. "Here goes. I've got this friend who is always on about conspiracy theories, you know? And he got me to thinking. And once I started thinking, well…I just can't get it out of my head."

"What is it, Manny?"

"Suppose…just suppose, there was this company. It's a successful company, but it's going through a bit of a tough time. Stretched a little thin, maybe. The boss is having health problems. It's not in the strongest position it could be in. You know what I mean?"

"This sounds suspiciously like Allman Industries," Jodie said.

"Yeah, well, whatever. Now, there is this guy who wants to buy the company. But the owner won't sell. So he worms his way into the company, gets people to trust him, looks for weakness. And then he gets a bright idea. He thinks he has a way to force the owner to sell by making the company weaker."

She went very still. "And what would that be?"

"Introduce some kind of weird disease into the vineyards, something that no one knows how to deal with."

"Manny…"

"Some kind of thing he can control later on, once he takes over the company. Something only he can handle."

"Manny!"

"The owner's going under, so he has to sell. And at a pretty good price, too. So the guy who wants to buy is sitting in the catbird seat."

Her fingers tightened on the receiver. "Manny, what exactly are you trying to say here?"

"You want it straight? I'm saying, once a McLaughlin, always a McLaughlin. And that's all I got to say about it. You tell Rafe. Okay?"

"But Manny, wait. I know you're talking about Kurt. What makes you think he wants to buy the company?"

"'Cuz he tried to buy it."

That hard, stinging fist was forming in her stomach again. "When?"

"When he first moved back here. That's how he got the job with your dad. He wanted to buy and your father said, 'No, but why don't you take a job with me instead?' So he did."

Jodie frowned. "Are you sure about that?"

"Absolutely. Rafe told me at the time."

Hanging up, she felt numb. This scenario would fit right in with her original suspicions about Kurt. But she'd gotten over those. Hadn't she?

No, this was just crazy. Manny was imagining things. Still, maybe she ought to talk to Rafe when he got back.

She bathed and fed Katy, and put her to bed for her nap. Watching her from the doorway, Jodie thought about her own pregnancy, and the hopes and dreams she'd had for her baby. Funny how knowing Katy had softened the sting of those memories. She hated to think that just loving a new baby would blot out all feeling for the lost one.

Suddenly her eyes filled with tears, and she knew that those old feelings would never completely disappear. There would always be a little piece of her heart that belonged to the baby who had been taken from her. But one did have to live life as one found it.

The phone rang again. She stared at it for a moment

before answering. This seemed to be a bad news day. She had a feeling she wasn't going to like what she found on the other end of the line.

A gruff man asked for Kurt and seemed perturbed when she told him about San Antonio.

"You his secretary? Okay, please take a message. Let him know that the loan is okayed, contingent on a face-to-face. They're an old-fashioned firm, and the paperwork is all okay, but with a major loan like this, they want to check him out personally before signing on the dotted line. They like to get the measure of the man, if you know what I mean. So if he could call and set up a meeting, that would be the ticket."

"I'll give him the message."

She wrote down the man's number and hung up, then sat back, her stomach churning. Kurt was taking out a major loan. Did this somehow fit in with Manny's crazy story?

Things started flooding back to her, things she'd pushed aside and ignored. She remembered what Tracy had said the other day when Jodie had overheard her arguing with Kurt. Something about Kurt restoring the family to its position in the town. And Kurt said something about how his family would understand what he was doing when it was all over. Why hadn't she dealt with what she'd heard before now?

Because she wanted to pretend she hadn't heard it.

She was such a fool. How could she have let herself fall for a McLaughlin—again?

Chapter Ten

It was late afternoon when Rafe dropped Kurt off in front of the house. Jodie was watching for him. The cast had been removed, and his walk was almost normal as he came up the path to the front porch. Watching him, she felt a surge of emotion. She loved this man. But what was she going to do? Should she confront him with her suspicions? Or go to Matt and Rafe? Either way was disloyal—either to her family, or to the man she loved.

She had her things gathered and her keys in her hand by the time he had the front door open. She had to find a place where she could think this through. And she couldn't stay here with Kurt any longer. After all, he wouldn't need her now. Though it broke her heart, she knew she needed to get away from his influence so that she could think.

She'd been right from the beginning. She should have known better than to get involved with Kurt and his baby. But she had known, hadn't she? And she'd tried to stay away. She'd known deep down that it would only lead to heartbreak. And that was exactly what had happened.

Kurt stared after Jodie as she hurried to her car. He had no idea what had upset her.

The expression on her face as she'd left wasn't a look of betrayal. He knew that look. He'd seen it in Grace's eyes often enough. It was seared in his memory.

No, Jodie's gaze had held the look of loss. A look of goodbye.

Not the sort of goodbye that Grace's face had mirrored. Not that sort of sneaky, furtive, I'm-going-to-cheat-on-you goodbye.

No, it was more an I-found-out-something-about-you-that-I-don't-like goodbye. Where had that come from?

Katy was crying. He went to her quickly and picked her up, holding her to his shoulder and murmuring comfort. She was all he had in the world, and he was all she had. But they both needed more. She felt precious in his arms, but she kept crying, sounding as though her heart would break. It wasn't like her to cry this way. She must be missing Jodie already. And maybe she felt the tension. He began to walk with her snuggled against his chest, stroking her back as he went. But his mind was consumed with Jodie, and that look in her eyes.

Funny how Jodie had always seemed to be lurking

somewhere in the back of his mind. From that day in the park as a little girl, when she'd thrown down the ice cream cone he offered her, she'd stuck in his consciousness like a burr. She was a puzzle, a mystery that beguiled him from afar. Then he'd seen her at that rodeo, in the red halter top, and sexual attraction had entered the picture, increasing his fascination. She was too young then, and he'd left her alone. He'd always thought that later, when she was older…

But she'd disappeared from Chivaree and he'd met Grace, and life had gone on. Still, when Jodie had walked into his office just over a month ago, those old feelings had flooded back. There had always been something about her that had captured his fancy, and that something was still going strong.

He was a different person now, of course. He'd experienced love and death and betrayal. He'd thought these things had taught him to keep a wall of protection around his heart. Never again would he let someone else rule his emotions. Even Jodie.

But when he'd seen the look in her eyes as she'd brushed past him this afternoon, his guts had begun to churn. What the hell could it be? What had set her off? He looked around the room, but the only thing he found was a note on the pad of paper by the telephone. Jodie must have taken a call and jotted down a message for him. He scanned it. Gerhard Briggs had called to tell him the loan was probably a go. Great. But that was the least of his worries now.

He stared at the note, at the clear, curved script of Jodie's handwriting. He loved that writing. She was so...so perfect. So perfect for him. Something stirred in his chest.

Had he lost her?

No. Unacceptable. He couldn't let her walk away.

The last few weeks had been the happiest of his life. Katy had brought him overwhelming joy, but Jodie, he knew with sudden conviction, could bring him inner peace. There was no one like her.

But what could he promise *her?*

He'd loved Grace once, too. That was what made him antsy about this whole love thing. Looking back now, he realized they had been strangers to each other long before Katy arrived on the scene and the breach between them became a canyon. The rift had begun years before, and accelerated once another man complicated things.

An old friend of Grace's had shown up on their doorstep a few months before Katy was born. He was checking out New York City and needed a place to stay for a few days, so Kurt offered him a bed in their apartment. A few days stretched into weeks. He was looking for a job, he'd said. He began hanging out with a crowd Kurt didn't like. Kurt had ordered him out.

Grace had been angry with him at the time, but she was on the verge of giving birth, and all wrapped up in the excitement, so he hadn't thought too much about it. Ah, hell. The truth was, he hardly paid any attention to

Grace anymore by then. He was excited about the baby, but Grace and her ups and downs had finally become so annoying, he pretty much tuned her out.

He had a lot to regret about his marriage. He certainly hadn't been a perfect husband, and there was a measure of guilt on his side. He could have worked harder at pleasing Grace, or at least, in understanding what it was that would please her. Somehow the love between them had turned to a sort of poison.

Did he love Jodie? And if he did, would it last longer than his love for Grace had lasted?

Putting Katy, now asleep, down in her crib, he paced his house restlessly. He wanted to go to Jodie. But what could he say? What could he offer her?

Suddenly, he knew. He checked his watch. It was getting late. He had to go out. But there was Katy. He had to find someone to stay with her. Maybe a neighbor…

The doorbell rang. Jodie was back, Kurt thought. His heart surged in his chest and he sprang to the door, ignoring the sharp flash of pain in his knee. Throwing it open, he found Manny Cruz on his doorstep.

"Listen, man," Manny said without preamble, jabbing an extended finger in his face. "I gotta talk to you."

Kurt's initial disappointment faded quickly. "Come on in, Manny," he said, turning back into the house and searching for his wallet. "Thank God you showed up. I need you." Manny could baby-sit. He was a baby expert.

"For what, man?" Manny bounced on his toes, looking loose. "Hey, come on back here. I called over here to fight you."

Kurt barely looked up. "What are you talking about?"

Manny stationed himself where Kurt couldn't ignore him. "I'm not going to let you steal the business from the Allmans, okay?" he said, trying to sound threatening. "I'm not going to let you ruin that great family. I finally figured out your game, and I'm going to be the one to stop you."

Exasperation filled Kurt, and he stopped, looking the shorter man in the face. "Manny, listen. I have no intention of ruining the Allman family, or taking their business away from them."

"Oh, yeah?" Manny's chin stuck out belligerently.

"Yeah."

"Then why are those dudes prowling around in the vineyards?"

"Those are graduate students in botany at the university. They're collecting more samples of the problem with the vines."

Manny's face changed. "Oh."

"I've talked to my old professor," Kurt said, finally finding his wallet and putting it into the back pocket of his jeans. "He thinks they might be able to come up with a diagnosis and some remedies we can try. He's pretty optimistic."

"So…you're not trying to ruin the crop?"

He stared at Manny, incredulous. "Why would I want to ruin the crop?"

"So you could buy the company cheaper."

Kurt blinked, then swore softly. "Manny, I'm not trying to buy the Allmans' company out from under them."

Manny frowned. "But you tried to buy it from the first."

"No, I didn't. I invested a good deal of money in it. That's true. And I'm taking out a loan to help pay for a couple of new bottling machines. I'm fully committed to this company. I think it's going to turn this town into a prosperous place. But it will always belong to the Allmans."

Manny frowned, digesting the news. "Hey, I guess I had you pegged all wrong," he said, his face turning a deep shade of red. "Sorry about that."

"No problem," Kurt said amicably.

Manny cleared his throat. "So you think they found a cure for my vines?"

"It's possible. I'm going to have my professor friend come out and talk to you soon."

Still intent on getting to Jodie as quickly as possible, he picked up his car keys and looked around the room to see if there was anything he was forgetting. "But right now, I've got a problem to take care of."

He stopped suddenly and frowned, turning to look at the other man as an unpleasant thought came to him. "Listen, Manny. Did you tell anyone else you suspected me of trying to take over the company?"

Manny nodded. "I came over here earlier. I was so upset. I only told Jodie, though. Hey, you gotta tell her I was wrong, okay?"

Kurt's face froze and his heart sank. So that was what

Jodie's strange mood was all about. "Sure," he said slowly. "Sure. I'll tell her." But he set his keys back down and changed his mind about asking Manny to watch Katy for him.

They talked for a few minutes and then Manny left. Kurt stayed where he was, staring into the gathering darkness. Had it really been so easy for Jodie to believe the worst of him? Just one rant from Manny and she'd turned against him. He was a McLaughlin, wasn't he? And therefore, not afforded a benefit of the doubt. Still, it was hard to believe she hadn't even thought to give him a chance to give his side of things. It was almost as if she'd jumped at an excuse to sever the ties. Maybe she was actually more like Grace than he'd known.

She was gone. He closed his eyes and faced the truth. Yes, she was gone. He wasn't going to go after her and beg her to come back. He knew from experience that sort of thing didn't work for long. It would only put off the ultimate agony.

And it did hurt. He'd thought he'd protected himself from ever feeling this sort of pain again, but here it was. And along with the pain came a deep, burning anger. How could she have been so ready to believe he was a liar and a cheat?

Maybe it was just as well. And certainly it was better that it happen now, before they'd made any sort of intimate commitment. But the thought that he might never kiss her again, or see her smile at him with that sunny joy in her eyes, cut like a knife.

Swearing softly, he looked out the window into the night. Maybe she'd been right from the beginning, and their relationship had always been doomed by that damned feud.

Jodie looked up and saw Kurt stepping off the elevator with a small group of others. Quickly, she looked back down at her work, but she couldn't stop her heart from beating wildly as it always did when she caught sight of him. He and the others passed by not far from where she sat at her desk, but she pretended to be engrossed in work.

It had been almost a week since she'd last been at Kurt's house and they hadn't had one real conversation. They had worked together every day, but only here at the office, and every word they'd spoken had been concerned with the job. At one point she'd been about to ask him how Katy was, but she'd overheard him telling Shelley that one of his ubiquitous cousins was taking care of the baby temporarily. So her own question was answered.

She hated this. She knew he was angry at the way she'd left. He knew she'd thought he was guilty of something. She also knew that the suspicions Manny had kindled in her that day were false. Matt and Rafe had both set her straight on that score, and she deeply regretted that she'd let herself fall into such a stupid mistake.

But things had gone beyond that now. The way she saw it, Kurt had taken the opportunity to dump her once he no longer needed her. He'd hinted it was coming when he'd told her she was getting too serious. After all, he'd told her from the beginning he wasn't in the market for a committed relationship. She'd gone into the whole thing knowing what she was risking. And she supposed she'd gotten what she deserved.

But that didn't stop her from crying herself to sleep at night. She was in love with the man. What could she do?

And then there was Katy. Sweet, dear little Katy. How she ached to hold that wiggly little body in her arms again! She'd gone from wanting nothing to do with children to loving one completely, in just a few days. Was it possible to change so quickly?

Yes, if fear was faced down.

Hmm. That was something that might bear further thought.

It was only a half hour later when Shelley stopped by her desk.

"Hey, your boss wants to see you in the boardroom."

"Do you mean Kurt?" she asked, looking up in surprise.

Shelley made a face at her. "Isn't he your boss?"

Of course he was, much as she'd tried to change that from the first. Rising, she took a deep breath and made her way to the boardroom. She assumed he had some comment to make on the advertising proposals she'd turned in that morning. They'd worked together so closely for a while, been so in tune with each other, it felt awkward to go back to being a plain old employee again. Still, it had to be done, and she was determined to be as bright and cheerful as possible.

"Good morning," she called out as she pushed open the heavy door to the boardroom and breezed in.

The room had recently been remodeled and it was now her father's pride and joy. One wall was lined with impressively ornate bookcases full of beautifully bound volumes, while the other was paneled in elegant mahogany and decorated with framed awards the company had won. The table was long and heavy and the chairs that lined it were richly upholstered.

Kurt was sitting at one end of the table, his auburn hair slightly longer than usual, as though he hadn't taken time for a haircut lately. There was a sense of expectation in his green eyes as they met hers. And then she noticed he was holding something in his lap. It took her a second or two to realize it was a child.

"Katy!" she cried out before she could stop herself.

The little tousled head turned and Katy squealed with delight.

"Ma ma!" she cried, throwing out her chubby arms toward Jodie. "Ma da ma da!"

Jodie ignored Kurt, ignored the nonsense syllables the baby was crying out, and reached for the little girl she'd so recently grown to love. Kurt didn't prevent her, and in no time at all she had Katy snuggled securely in her arms. She cooed loving sounds to her, kissing her round cheeks and laughing along with the child.

"Did you hear that?" Kurt said casually. "She called you Mama. Does that bother you?"

She turned to look down into his handsome face. His

gaze was unreadable, but something in the air made her heartbeat start to race again.

"Kurt, what are you trying to do to me?" she asked him.

He shrugged and a slight smile twitched at the corners of his mouth.

"I'm just exploring the idea of you being a mother. What do you think? Is there a possibility you could warm to the role?"

She stared at him, forgetting to breathe. "What?" she said, groping for context. "Are you talking about hiring me again?"

Before he could answer, Shelley came in with some papers and Kurt rose, taking Katy from Jodie's arms and handing her to Shelley.

"Can you take her down to the lunchroom and give her an ice cream or something?" he asked.

"Sure." Shelley looked from one to the other of them with a smirk. "We'll have a great time, won't we Katy?"

Jodie's gaze was still locked with Kurt's as Shelley and Katy disappeared.

"Sit down," he said.

She slid carefully into the seat beside his and waited for him to begin.

It took him a moment. He seemed to be collecting his thoughts. And then he turned to her again.

"I've been doing a lot of thinking over the last few days," he said.

She nodded. "Me, too," she admitted softly.

"I've been an idiot."

Looking quickly into his eyes, she tried to read his meaning. Was he regretting their rift? Or was he sorry they'd ever gotten so close? It was hard to tell. But there was one thing she was sure of.

"You're still angry with me."

He hesitated, frowning. "A little," he admitted.

She ran her tongue over her dry lips and pressed on. "Why exactly?"

A look of pain flashed over his face. "Because you didn't trust me. I thought you had gotten to know me pretty well, and still you had no faith in me."

Her heart sank, but she couldn't leave him with that impression. Because suddenly she realized it wasn't really true.

"No," she said earnestly. "That wasn't it. Don't you see? I had no faith in *myself*. I…I was scared, and I needed some time, some space to think things over. When all these signs seemed to point to you betraying the company, I…okay, it did upset me. And I sort of used that as an excuse to run away."

He nodded slowly. "But that still doesn't answer my basic question. You fell for it too easily, Jodie." The color of his eyes seemed to deepen. "Was it me? Or was it that stupid feud?"

She looked down at her hands, gripped tightly in her lap. Then she looked up again. "The feud is still there, still a part of me. I'm going to have to work very hard to get rid of it. But Kurt…" She bit her lip, then went on. "Kurt, I will get rid of it. I'll erase it from my system. I know I can do it."

Reaching out, he took one of her hands in his, lacing their fingers together. "So you don't think I'm trying to cheat your family?"

She closed her eyes for a second. "Oh, Kurt..."

"Because I'm not, you know."

"I know." She winced, looking guilty. "Rafe explained to me how you've been bankrolling things for Pop for months now. That if it hadn't been for you, the company would have gone under by now."

"Well, I don't know about that, but..."

"I just have to say one thing," she said, determined now to get this all out while she still had the courage to do so. She squeezed his fingers tightly. "I just want you to know. I love you, Kurt McLaughlin."

There. She'd said it and she braced herself, not sure what to expect. Would he get that wary look on his face and draw back and start talking about her getting too serious again? She held her breath, waiting.

He looked astonished. Then, slowly, he began to smile. Leaning toward her, he slid his free hand into the hair at the back of her head and began pulling her closer.

"Do you know how much I've missed kissing you?" he said huskily.

"Oh!" She put a hand on his chest to hold him back. "We can't kiss here. It's the boardroom."

"Hey, you forget. I'm the boss. I can conduct this meeting anyway I want to." He grinned at her. "And I say, when love's involved, kissing is mandatory."

She still held him off. "Does that mean…?"

"What? You want me to say the words?"

She nodded hopefully.

"Okay. Here they are. I love you, Jodie Allman. Though I'm planning to change that last name of yours as soon as possible."

She laughed, but not for long. His mouth covered hers and she melted against him, soaking up his tenderness and returning it in kind. Joy shimmered through her. She could hardly believe her dreams could come true this way. Drawing back, she smiled at him, her lips tingling.

"Oh, Kurt, I'm so sorry I put you through all that. You didn't deserve the distrust."

"No. Actually, I didn't." He grinned, touching her cheek, his love shining in his green eyes. "No more feud, okay?"

She held up her hand. "I swear. No more feud."

They smiled into each other's eyes, feeling like lovebirds.

And then Kurt pulled her close again. "Listen, Jodie," he said with sudden urgency. "Are you going to marry me and be the mother of my children or not?"

"I don't know. This is all so sudden."

"The hell it is. I've been looking at you since I could barely shave and you were jailbait. It's time we put some closure to this thing."

Tilting her head back, she searched his eyes and was happy with what she saw there. "You do mean it?"

"Cross my heart."

She sighed. "Oh, I do love you!"

"I love you, too, Jodie."

"Oh." Tears glistened in her eyes.

"So. Will you or won't you? Say yes."

She smiled up at him. "Yes. Oh, yes!"

"Good."

And he kissed her again, just to seal the bargain.

* * * * *

*In Raye Morgan's next Silhouette Romance,
turnabout is fair play.... Sparks fly when Rafe Allman
grudgingly switches roles with his sassy secretary in
TRADING PLACES WITH THE BOSS.*

*Watch for this delightful second installment of
BOARDROOM BRIDES in March 2005!*

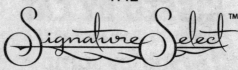
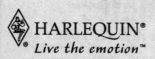

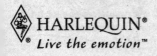

COMING NEXT MONTH

#1754 NIGHTTIME SWEETHEARTS—Cara Colter
In a Fairy Tale World...

She never forgot the brooding bad boy who had, once upon a time, made her heart race. So when Cynthia Fosythe hears a husky, familiar voice calling to her out of the tropical moonlit night she's stunned. She'd let go of Rick Barnett to preserve her good-girl image, but now Cynthia's prepared to lay it all on the line for another chance at paradise.

#1755 INSTANT MARRIAGE, JUST ADD GROOM—
Myrna Mackenzie

Nortorious bachelor Caleb Fremont is just what baby-hungry Victoria Holbrook is looking for—the perfect candidate for the father of her child. Although Caleb isn't interested in being a dad, he's agreed to a temporary marriage of convenience. But when the stick finally turns pink will he be able to let Victoria—and his baby—go?

#1756 DADDY, HE WROTE—Jill Limber

Reclusive author Ian Miller purchased an historic farmhouse to get some much-needed peace and quiet—and overcome his writer's block. Yet when he finds that the farm comes complete with beautiful caretaker Trish Ryan and her delightful daughter, Ian might find that inspiration can be found in the most unlikely places....

#1757 KISSED BY CAT—Shirley Jump
Soulmates

When Garrett McCallister discovers a purr-fectly gorgeous woman in his veterinary clinic, wearing nothing but a lab coat, he's confused, suspicious...and very intrigued. Will Garrett run when he discovers Catherine Wyndham's secret curse, or will he let the mysterious siren into his heart?

SRCNM0105